PUBLISHER'S NOTE

MANY of Ezra Pound's contributions to modern literature appeared originally in little magazines, in pamphlets, and in books which went quickly out of print. The present collection has been made in order to bring before the public today works which have been difficult to obtain for many years. Some pieces in this book are published here for the first time, most have been taken from a variety of out-of-the-way sources, and a very few, reprinted from Mr. Pound's other well known collections, have been included because they seem in keeping with the spirit of the rest. In general, the collection offers an aspect of Mr. Pound's work which is not to be found in other currently available publications, and thus helps to complete the record.

PAVANNES
AND
DIVAGATIONS

BY EZRA POUND

ABC OF READING
THE CANTOS OF EZRA POUND (NUMBERS 1–117 & 120)
THE CLASSIC NOH THEATRE OF JAPAN
COLLECTED EARLY POEMS OF EZRA POUND
CONFUCIUS (ENGLISH VERSIONS)
CONFUCIUS TO CUMMINGS (WORLD POETRY ANTHOLOGY)
EZRA POUND AND DOROTHY SHAKESPEARE 1909–1914:
THEIR LETTERS
EZRA POUND AND MUSIC
EZRA POUND AND THE VISUAL ARTS
GAUDIER-BRZESKA
GUIDE TO KULCHUR
LITERARY ESSAYS
LOVE POEMS OF ANCIENT EGYPT (TRANSLATED WITH NOEL STOCK)
PAVANNES AND DIVAGATIONS
PERSONAE
POUND/FORD: THE STORY OF A LITERARY FRIENDSHIP
POUND/JOYCE: LETTERS & ESSAYS
POUND/LEWIS: THE LETTERS OF EZRA POUND AND WYNDHAM LEWIS
POUND/ZUKOFSKY: SELECTED LETTERS OF EZRA POUND AND LOUIS ZUKOFSKY
SELECTED CANTOS
SELECTED LETTERS 1907–1941
SELECTED PROSE 1909–1965
SELECTED POEMS
THE SPIRIT OF ROMANCE
TRANSLATIONS
WOMEN OF TRACHIS (SOPHOKLES)

EZRA POUND

PAVANNES
AND
DIVAGATIONS

A NEW DIRECTIONS BOOK

Parts of this book have been previously published as follows, and
the author and Publisher are grateful for the right to republish them
here: Indiscretions, or Une Revue de Deux Mondes, by Ezra Pound,
William Bird, Three Mountains Press, Paris, 1923; Imaginary Letters,
by Ezra Pound, The Black Sun Press, Paris, 1930; "Jodindranath
Mawhwor's Occupation," "An Anachronism at Chinon," "Religio,
or the Child's Guide to Knowledge," "Aux Etuves de Wiesbaden,"
"Stark Realism," and "Twelve Dialogues of Fontenelle" from Pavannes
and Divisions, Alfred A. Knopf, New York, 1918 (Copyright 1918,
R 1944 by Ezra Pound); "Madox Ford at Rapallo" from Mood, No.
24, Fall 1950, St. Louis, Mo.; "A Matter of Modesty" from Esquire,
May 1935, Chicago; Alfred Venison's Poems published originally in
The New English Weekly, Vol. IV, No. 18 to Vol. VI, No. 2, Febru-
ary to November 1934, London. Republished as one of the "Pam-
phlets on the New Economics" by Stanley Nott, Ltd., 1935, London;
"Genesis, or, The First Book in the Bible" and "Our Tetrarchal
Precieuse" from Instigations, by Ezra Pound, Boni and Liveright,
New York, 1920 (Copyright 1920, R 1948 by Ezra Pound); "Post-
script" from The Natural Philosophy of Love, by Remy de Gourmont,
(trans. by Ezra Pound), Black and Gold Library, by permission of
Liveright Publishing Corp., New York (Copyright 1922 Liveright,
Inc.; R 1949 Liveright Publishing Corp.); "Musicians: God Help
'Em," "M. Pom-Pom," and "Abu Salammamm—A Song of Empire"
from Townsman, Vol. 1, No. 4, Vol. 1, No. 1, Vol. 2, No. 5, October
1938, January 1938, January 1939; (London); "Mr. Housman's
Message," "The New Cake of Soap," "Ancient Music," and "Our
Contemporaries," from Personae, the Collected Poems of Ezra
Pound, New Directions, New York (Copyright 1926 by Ezra Pound,
R 1954 by Ezra Pound); the translations of Saturna Montanari were
first published in Imagi, Vol. 5, No. 3, 1951, and are reprinted with
the permission of its editor, Thomas Cole.

Manufactured in the United States of America.
Published simultaneously in Canada by Penguin Books Canada Limited.
First published as New Directions Paperbook 397
(ISBN: 0-8112-0575-4) in 1975.

New Directions Books are published for James Laughlin
by New Directions Publishing Corporation,
80 Eighth Avenue, New York 10011.

SECOND PRINTING

EPITAPH

Here he lies, the Idaho kid,
The only time he ever did.

Rex Lampman

CONTENTS

INDISCRETIONS
or, Une Revue De Deux Mondes

HERMIONE

INDISCRETIONS
or, Une Revue De Deux Mondes

IT is peculiarly fitting that this manuscript should begin in Venice, from a patent Italian inkwell designed to prevent satisfactory immersion of the pen. If the latter symbolism be obscure, the former is so obvious, at least to the writer, that only meticulous honesty and the multitude of affairs prevented him from committing it to paper before leaving London.

Whereafter two days of anaesthesia, and the speculation as to whether, in the development and attrition of one's faculties, Venice could give one again and once more either the old kick to the senses or any new perception; whether coming to the belief that human beings are more interesting than anything possible else—certainly than any possible mood of colours and footlights-like glare-up of reflection turning house-façades into stage card-board; whether in one's anthropo- and gunaikological passion one were wise to leave London itself—with possibly a parenthetical Paris as occasional watch-tower and alternating exotic *mica salis;* and whether—the sentence being the mirror of man's mind, and we having long since passed the stage when "man sees horse" or "farmer sows rice," can in simple ideographic record be said to display anything remotely resembling our subjectivity—and whether—to exhaust a few more semicolons and dashes—one would—will, now that I am out of a too cramped room at the Albergo Bella Venezia and into a much too expensive one at this hostel which bears the hyphenated conjunction of a beer (Pilsen) and of the illustrious—but to the outer world somewhat indefinite saviour of his country, Manin [1]—whether the figures in the opposite windows of the Cavaletto—à la Matisse—with faces that *ought* to be painted à la Matisse, a streak of nose and two blobs of eye-shadows—adequate recognition, presumably, of their claim to individual existence; or the Kirchner cuts emerging from the archway from the Piazza S. Marco, and skirting the Bacino Orseolo and thence progressing, inspectably from my window and balcony, along the Fondamenta Orseolo; or the possible "picturesque" of roof-tiles, sky-tones, mud-green tidal influx, cats perched like miniature stone lions on balconies, etc., is going to afford a possible interest—after all that has been "done" about Venice; and whether the Kirchners—let us say the female who advances with just the least suggestion of being at guard in a fencing match, the knees seeming to be just slightly, yet obviously, in advance of the rest of her person, her attendant being and remaining both on the way to, and on the return from the Piazza, about half a pace to the rear; or the exaggerated turban, or the transparent very wide hat brim, united, all three, by a certain thinness of tone, not, let us say, an exaggerated preoccupation with their basic unmaleness, but by a consciousness of this fact outweighing any possible modifications of that consciousness by the personal element, as if, indeed, the whole of their mental content might be emptied out of the current number of "Femina," or even of some Roumanian publication illustrated and produced on that model, for gratuitous distribution in Sleeping Cars.

[1] Fragility of local glory only too evident in the fact that the first reprobatory British proofreader effaced this Venetian name and substituted that of Mazzini.

Or whether, in place of these very general observations
from this altitude—to augment my collection of human
forminifera I shouldn't have stayed in London, where, in
the vastly greater concurrence of specimens, one has so
much better a chance of finding a "good one," a higher
demarcation, a wider divergence from human cliché.

However: Venice, Der alte Venezia, with lurking sus-
picions that the cursed noun is feminine and demands a
different approach, but that the sometimes sentimental
tone of the Harzreise must be recalled to oneself if not
to the reader, and that some sort of salvo must be allowed
the habitat where one's first recueil was printed—for it
is, after all, an excellent place to come to from Craw-
fordsville, Indiana, whatever it may be as a point of arrival from London—with the old gardens of the Rue
Jacob as intermediate impression, and with San Bertrand
de Comminges, and Rocafixada fresher in the mind than
any inculte circumjacence.

Let it therefore stand written that I first saw the Queen
of the Adriatic under the protection of that portentous
person, my great aunt-in-law, in the thirteenth year of
my age; and that my European inceptions had begun a
few weeks earlier with the well-donkey at Carisbrooke
Castle, and very large strawberries served with "Devon-
shire cream" at Cowes, and that the chances are I had
"seen" Paris, Genoa, Rome, Naples, Florence, and probably the leaning towers of Bologna (these last from the
train) in the interval. Or it is possible that I had not
"seen" Paris, but Brussels, Cologne, Mainz, Nuremberg.
The exact order of these impressions, seeing that I was
to revisit half of them four years later, is now somewhat
difficult to recall; and I do not know whether I have been
twice, or been only once in Pisa.

My "Great Aunt" had, however, danced with General
Grant. She believed that travel broadened the mind. I am
unable to record its effect upon her own cerebration; I
know that at the instance of her nieces, who owed, or

should, on this theory, have owed, a part of their mental
latification to her purse and incentive, she consented to
admit that the one adjective, beautiful, was not univer-
sally applicable to all European phenomena, from Alps
to San Marco and Titians (or even Murillos) and to the
glass filagrees of Murano; but she continued to use it,
with apologies. And her wide and white-bodiced figure—
as for example perched on a very narrow mule in Tan-
giers—is an object of pious memory as she herself is of
gratitude. Without her I might not have been here. Venice struck me as an agreeable place—as, in fact, more
agreeable than Wyncote, Pa., or "47th" and Madison Avenue. I announced an intention to return. I have done so.
I do not know quite how often. By elimination of possible years: 1898, 1902, 1908, 1910, 1911, 1913, 1920.

2

It is one thing to feel that one could write the whole social history of the United States from one's family annals,
and vastly another to embark upon any such Balzacian
and voluminous endeavour. Hence my great-aunt in
parenthesis; hence Joseph Wadsworth, who stole the
Connecticut charter and hid it in Charter Oak, to the
embarrassment of legitimist tyranny: picturesque circumstances, candles snuffed out with a cloak which popular
art has represented as cavalier rather than roundhead;
hence also Israel Putnam, who until recently in multi-
tudinous tramcars galloped down his two hundred stone
steps with his back towards his horse's head and his face
(alarms, huzzahs, excursions)—his face to the enemy:
for the purposes then present of commerce and the ré-
clame of a modern whiskey which we presume never
turned *its* back on an enemy.

There is also an heraldic ornament (described at some
length in Longfellow's "Tales of a Wayside Inn,") with
which my childhood was early familiar. *Il y a aussi le*

costume historique. A la mi-carême. We are all, in the words of Æsop, descended from Jove, and if our ancestors are an influence, one can only suppose that in their geometric progression from two to sixty-four and thence on to egregious numbers and remoteness, the exact bearing of a given and deceased x^n upon a given and living x^m is subject for the sentimental romanticist. Or perhaps it may be held that the actions of one's ancestors, especially if recited to one in childhood, tend to influence one's character and materially to exhaust one's interest in a given subject or subjects.

Given, then, that there may have been a certain intellectual interest in stealing charters pro bono (very romantically) publico; or in participating in the Sinn Fein of '76; or in elaborate misrepresentations of descent from men who had curried favour with such unestimable monarchs as Edward II and Charles II; or in timber, horse-fodder, mines, railways, ranching, agriculture, I might reasonably say that I had received personal and confidential reports on these matters at a very early age and that my interest had suffered etiolation.

A certain amount of bait is swallowed by all of us; familiar consciousness or even elderly garrulity may prevent one from swallowing bait which has already been taken by one's immediate forebears.

Etiolated (ref., two paragraphs higher), that is, to the extent that one had no intention of allowing these things to obtrude upon one's own future action, even though one may in the safety of twenty years' lapse, and from the security of the Albergo Pilsen-Manin—or even from Kensington, W.—admit their value as literary capital—in part. And, in other part too fully exploited, to the extent that "America," that egoistic portion which usurps the name of the whole and views with surprised entertainment any Castilian effort to distinguish: "*Los Estados Unidos de América, Señor? O los Estados Unidos de Brasil?*" for the avoidance of ambiguity: the land of the

Star-spangled Banner appears to have passed through an era of unmixed motives, recorded with *simplesse* in the school histories of thirty years ago, and in the almost equally simple versification of Longfellow. One cannot in the face of this, therefore, "do" anything more with Paul Revere, or with the spire of Old North Church, save possibly climb the interior of said spire and be vastly startled by the extremely proximate roar of its bells— when at precocious age, visiting the Massachusetts centre of culture, to attend a Christian Endeavour convention.

My father, the naïvest man who ever possessed sound sense, and whose virtues have more than once served him as well as, or possibly better than, other men are served by intellectual subtlety, was at that time, I believe, interested in the prospects of an earnest young C. E. worker who has since attained no small publicity by journalising the Bible; by serving up this old dish weekly with a new sauce of headlines, as "DANIEL SURROUNDED BY LIONS, *Famous Hebrew Prophet* comes safe from monarch's menagerie"; or "ZACCHEUS IN THE BRANCHES, climbs tree to observe procession and IS NOTICED BY WORLD'S REDEEMER."

As a demonstration that there is life in the old book yet, we mention that this "news treatment" of sacred story ran for a number of years in a leading Philadelphia Sunday edition, and may, for all I know to the contrary, be still "like Johnny Walker"—and syndicated at that. Father was right, as usual, in his central proposition that "W.T." was "going to do something."

Colonial America has left a few anecdotes, heroic or bigoted; *il y a aussi le costume historique;* Fenimore Cooper, Irving, and possibly more illuminating than either, Jefferson as found in his now published private correspondence. There follow Hawthorne, who is excellent, if rather specialized, pleading; the somewhat distressing efforts at Concord, and the supreme portraiture in "Memories of a Small Boy and Others." Apart from what James has told us, we are fairly ignorant of vast patches of dated atmosphere: Why, for instance, my Great Aunt, or, to be exact, the lady whose middle husband was my bushy side-whiskered Great Uncle, should have danced at every "Inaugural" for a vast period of years, and why, having passed the span allotted this pleasure, she should have journeyed regularly to Washington to shake hands with the newly elected President —even, I think to shake Cleveland's, "who drank"—as regularly as she attended Dr. Parkhurst's or St. Bartholomew's on the Sabbath, or journeyed to Europe in June with a vast collection of valises, suit-cases, hold-alls, bandboxes, and heterogeneous parcels, I do not know. I know that for three months' travel there were ninety-seven little tissue-paper parcels of green tea prepared in advance and distributed throughout her multifarious luggage—ever since the painful occasion when they had all been found together on the top of *one* suit-case, to the amazement of a *douane* official.

I remember the effects of these little parcels, rather resembling "curl-papers," upon an assorted set of head waiters, the pompous, the confidential, the bewildered; but I have no idea what sort of people attended "Inaugurals" or danced at "Inaugurals" in the 'sixties, 'seventies, 'eighties. Henry James does not mention the function; he indicates that by 1890 or 1900 the President was no longer the centre of America's gravity, but from the nature of his indication and indeed from the correlation of the rest of his writings I am unable to make out whether any member of the James family ever attended an Inaugural; whether they would have considered it suitable—even in the vaguer and less critical "seventies," or whether they had simply not heard of the function. Henry James, Sr., had, as we know, intellectual interests which would have divided him from the community.

The New York "wharves," which H. J. records as heaped with water-melons and bushel-baskets of peaches, must have been not too unlike the old fruit market and other seemingly endless "Covent Gardens" on the west side "down town," to which I was taken by my Great Uncle, and, after his death, by my Great Aunt in the search for advantageous provisions. I remember a man throwing a large jack-knife some fifty feet after a fleeing male figure. The incident was unique so far as I was concerned, but seemed to arouse no curiosity among the by-standers.

James corraborates the statement that 14th Street was a proper street for the natal residence of one's mother, and I remember one of the "old" 23rd Street houses with two-storey porches set far back from the pavement, with long "front-yards," being pointed out to me as "owned" by the family in some rather legendary and possibly brief period of better-off-ness. This block or these blocks of houses, I forget how far "west" in 23rd Street, have or had somewhat the air of a forgotten London crescent and remained a sort of island of rural urbanity antedating the brown-stone, high-porched New York.

Francis Train still sat white-headed, or with, I think, a stiff straw hat on the back of his head, in a plain wooden hemicycular chair on the pavement before some hotel whereof the name escapes me. I was told that he was Francis Train; the statement conveyed nothing what-ever; even now I know nothing of him save that he was a "figure" and a publicist, and I have read that in the days before Christian Endeavour he had been jailed for publishing the Scriptures unexpurgated in a "paper," not, however, *pour le bon motif*, but in order to test the pudi-bundicity laws of his country. He may have been a friend of "Bob Ingersoll."

3

My grandfather, ultimately the Hon. Thadeus Cuthber-ton Weight, was born in the town of Elk, Warren County,

Pa., son of Ezekiel, son of Ezekiel, son of Ezekiel, of Ezekiel, for in this prænomen they had begotten each other in four stages from 1712 to 1812 anno domini, in the Quaker religion, and in the first instance in New Jersey from a Weight, reputedly a whaler. The American doomsday books or emigration records yield three Weights—two to Connecticut or Rhode Island in the 1630's, and one, "with body servant," to East Shore, Virginia, in, I think, 1638, from which attended arriver sprang, I presume, the "southern Weights," for one of whom I was once cordially received by mistake.

Thadeus, in first and legitimate espousals, took to himself Selina of the family Loomis, who were reputedly horse-thieves. That is to say, the family tradition, with the rather non-committal "India inks" of the genealogical Bible, reported them to have been county judges and that like in Upper New York State; but an old lady whom I met in Oneida County said they were horse thieves, charming people, in fact, the "nicest" people in the county, but horse-thieves, very good horse-thieves, never, I think, brought to book. She had met one of the younger members, and liked him extremely.

I cannot recall that this grandmother has ever mentioned her family. She once mentioned working in a mill after some crisis or other. If the family stole horses I am certain that no legal machinery would have extracted "any change out of her." At the age of 160 she and *her* mother, who must have been by that time 180 (exactitude is no matter when one reaches these legendary numbers), lived in Montana, not together, but each alone in her cabin with a good two miles of veldt between them. From her presumably I derive my respect for the human being as an individual, my dislike of herding, and of the encroachment of one personality upon another in the sty of the family.

I can remember no phrase of hers save that once in a discussion of conduct, she said: "Harve was *like* that."

The statement ended the matter. The Italian "*Così son io*," is a priceless heritage from the renaissance, but it is egocentric and possibly inferior to my grandmother's recognition of the demarcation and rights of personality.

Thadeus taught school; was expert in penmanship; "took up," as I believe from copy of a manual found in our trunkroom (*Anglicè*, boxroom) phrenology; also spiritualism; had some credit for the healing touch, and performed, I believe, in company with his brother Albert, a tour of spiritual or magnetic healing and demonstration; all of which goes to show that while Henry James was having his so modulated breakfasts in Half Moon Street, and irritating Gustave Flaubert, and, on the whole, acquiring just the right tone, the picaresque novel was still being lived in the less tonal or "toney" parts of his fatherland.

And if mediæval culture was sporadic and unorganized, I have also the "India inks" of the juridical horse-thieves to show that at least one artist had in the wilderness attained no inconsiderable proficiency. Whether this form of portraiture was due to lack of ivory for miniature, I do not know, but the technique is that of the excellent miniature school; the heads are unsigned. I have no means of judging whether they are all of one date; whether of one artist on tour, or whether this ink was a recognised and widely used medium. Farther to the east there existed Wm. Page, a painter, who, if my memory of one portrait serves me, must have been as good as, say, Raeburn, and who painted rather in the *olivâtre* tones of Van Dyke.

Thadeus ascended into lumbering; had, that is, a store from which he ministered to the material needs of Scandinavians employed by him to thin out virgin forests of Wisconsin. Companies of this sort paid all or part of their wages in token coinage good only in the company's "store." Thadeus entered these regions before cultural pressure was very great; aborigines still strolled through

the settlement at Minnehaha; my father had one for a
nurse. Thadeus appears to have amassed and disamassed
considerable sums of money at one period or another. He
undoubtedly fostered the advance of civilisation, had his
name in large brass letters on the front of a locomotive;
was probably president of the Wisconsin railway or some
such corporation, owning enough track to insure himself
and family "free passes" over all other then existing
American railroads.

"Logging," I take it, requires about beaver's intelligence; and like most other "rough" life and menial occupations, presents no interest that detains any higher
intelligence over a fortnight; it, like other labour, is performed by servile classes, or by men who simply haven't
the brains to do anything else without intolerable mental
fatigue, a mental fatigue more torturing than that of the
body. Trees are felled, large logs dragged to the water's
edge, tangle or "jam," often with ice as a complication,
require a certain technique in their disentanglement; are
or were bound into large rafts, and floated down stream
to saw-mills or shipping points. The lumberman was reputed to perform marvels of *legerdepied*, standing up-
right upon the single floating log and driving it, guiding
it backward and forward through the water by strokes of
his spiked boots.

It is observed in somebody or other's "Dawn of Civilisation," that man in flat graminiferous countries exists as
a parasite upon grass-eating animals, and it is to be noted
that the English race in America having eliminated the
"Red" race, has been successively a parasite upon the
black and upon the Continental European races. The
one pull against this has been Hodge's stubborn attach-
ment to the soil, to "property" in the form of New England and other farms. Lumbering was assigned to the
Swedes and Norwegians, as cotton and tobacco to the
negro, or steel to Croats, Slovenes and Hungarians; day
labour with pick and shovel to the Italians, with an Irish-

man as gang-boss. Twenty years ago I have even seen a negro as gang-boss over Italians.

Thadeus undoubtedly led a certain number of it into Wisconsin, laid railways that the suction might be facilitated, was himself filled with enthusiasms, or beliefs in the future, was elected to Congress, thus becoming "The Honourable"; took to himself a second feminine adjunct, without sanction of clergy.

She is reported to have been amiable and to have been "good to" my father during some period of stress, presumably financial. Thadeus became lieutenant and acting governor of Wisconsin; he presided with some vigour over the sessions of the State legislature or senate, and is known to have dissolved that body upon the instigation of some presumably supernatural agent, as no one else in assembly saw or heard either the mover or seconder of the motion.

Entering Congress a "rich man," he "left it a poor one" —though I have never been able to learn exactly what prodigy of rectitude these opposed statements may have, in their sequence, implied; America being a country where there is, seemingly, no limit to degree in which any fact or facts may abstain from implying anything, absolutely *any* thing else whatsoever. Thadeus, as we have said, served his State for three terms in the national Congress. The "Atlantic Monthly" devoted a serious article to his "prospects"; Garfield promised him a place in his cabinet if elected. But Garfield had made numerous promises, one notably to J. G. Blaine, who, in the event, declined "to sit in the same cabinet with a man who was not living with his wife." Mr. Blaine was the "bigger man" and the domestic proprieties of high official circles were preserved for the time being. Garfield was in due time shot by a less placid seeker of office, and succeeded by Chester A. Arthur, "one of the finest gentlemen who ever sat in the White House." This finesse was apparently

antipathetic to "bigness"; at any rate Mr. Blaine was the
next Republican nominee for the highest magistracy of
the nation. At this point, however, the impassive Thadeus
intervened in his career even more effectively than he
had four years previous intervened in that of Thadeus.
Wisconsin and several other Western States did not "go
Republican." Grover Cleveland ("who drank") was
elected, and had, I presume, an Inaugural. Both Blaine
and Thadeus passed permanently from the national political limelight.

Thadeus thus bequeathed to his son, my father, the
naive Euripides Weight, a certain sophistication, a certain ability to stand unabashed in the face of the largest
national luminaries, to reduce the objections of doorkeep-
ers and minor functionaries, to pass the "ropes," etc., designed for restricting democratic ingress and demoralis-
ing the popular enthusiasm at processions. He, Thadeus,
had, we believe, seriously contributed to the welfare of
certain localities. He left some permanent work in plans
for irrigation of the Western desert, made effective a
score of years after his agitation. He had opposed "nepotism" with the one palpable result of not having
pushed Euripides into a soft Washington job. He owned
in latter 'eighties a few silver mines in "The Rockies"
which were "jumped," and fell into a litigation which
was finally decided in his favour too late for the decision
to be of any use whatsoever. He owned still a farm, but
the fad for clipping the horns of milk-cows exercised
maleficent influence upon both the farm and the milk-
route. He retained even then a spring of the purest water
known to man, christened "laughing water" after Hia-
watha's beloved.

The ability to regard possibilities rather than facts
which had served him in foreseeing a wilderness ir-
rigated, still assisting him, he continued to see "millions
in it." Powdered alum caused no precipitation of sedi-

ment in the water of Chippewa spring; no other liquid would, or for I know will yet, stand this rigorous catechism.

The palpable results were a few cases of the by-products, ginger-ale and cherry-phosphate, supplied free from the factory, but with cartage charges (1,800 miles) which ineffected any economy. There lay also in our cellars two cases of the fat two-quart bottles of water; it was uninteresting, it tasted only like water.

Thadeus remained, I believe, an excellent conversationalist to the end. At his death the State legislature passed commemorative and complimentary resolutions.

4

THE little Euripides, son of Thadeus, son of Ezekiel, etc., was probably the first white male child born in the northern part of Wisconsin. He had, as we have indicated, an aborigine for nurse; he showed no evil impulses; his curious prænomen, diverging from the scriptural tradition of the house, was a pure tribute to the classics. One of Ezekiel's brothers read Greek. Ezekiel had ridden behind the first locomotive. Joel lived to be ninety-six, hale to the end and he "looked after" the younger and weaker Ezekiel, three years his junior.

This residue out of a lot of thirteen resided "at the end," presumably in parasitic capacity, on "the farm," whereof the large central building had a slate mansard roof encompassed by a cast-iron railing. Of the other ten brethren no fact is recorded, nor have they left traceable issue. This may have been the swing of the pendulum.

Apart from his admiration of the warm and human dripper of tears, no other fact is known of Uncle Joash. Euripides did not "take to" the new learning; his name's augury did not work. He retained four words of the Chippewa dialect: *Boudju nichisinn, we wipp,* of which the

first appears to be a corruption of the French-Canadian
bon jour.

He had a boat on the river, guarded by a pet gander;
there was no other boat-guarding gander in Wisconsin.
With the advance of civilisation he learned to drive his
father's racehorses. His sister was told to acquire accom-
plishments and provided with a 500 dol. harp for the
purpose. The primeval forest was receding. Euripides
collected thirty-seven photographs (carte-de-visite size)
of thirty-seven young ladies resident in Eau Claire. He
had his tin-type taken in company with the then Ella
Wheeler, later to delight two continents with her melody.
The "tin-type" was a cheap and festal photographic process which had then superseded the earlier and subtler
modus of Daguerry (for which refer Nathaniel Hawthorne's enthusiasm). Ella is seated on an artificial tree-
stump, before a factitious stile upon which Euripides
leans in a disingenuous manner.

Euripides drove a buggy, without which conveyance
America seemingly could not, in the seventies and eighties of the last century, have existed.[1] He had left one
school on the cow-catcher of an engine; he was placed in
the military school at Shattuck, Minnesota, and ultimately assigned to West Point. Appointments to this institution are not easily obtainable. Euripides, however,
having been spared all participation in the struggle, declined the laurel informally. That is to say, his family
placed him on the train, and he, for the first time specu-
lating on the advantages of the nation's finest and most
efficient military and mathematical education, "got off
half-way" and returned to his natal State. It was a perfectly sensible proceeding; he had no intention of com-
manding either a platoon or an army. Thadeus, shortly
after, went "bust." Euripides, wanting pocket-money, was
discovered at work in the butcher shop, presumably some

[1] The name of the vehicle is sometimes spelled also "boghey."

residuum or development of the "store" which had supplied the needs of the lumbermen. Thadeus disapproved
of Euripides' materialism, but Euripides remained at
work at least long enough to acquire that sound knowledge of crude edibles which enhanced his table later in
life.

Proximately, in about the twenty-fourth year of his
age, he must have taken to "hanging round" in Washington.

The careful stylist would presumably pause here for
some time. My great Aunt had, we remember, the habit
of invading Washington at regular intervals; whether she
encountered Euripides definitely in the act of grasping
some newly-found President by the hand, or whether in
an hotel or boarding-house, or in some more formal and
modulated encounter, I am uncertain; the problem being
rather the infusion of this unsorted, heteroclite frontier
life plus the wash of officialdom into the Jamesian atmosphere of New York, whither Euripides journeyed in my
great-aunt's somewhat voluminous wake, and upon a possibly somewhat sketchy invitation. Of Wisconsin it may
be postulated that it was not in Henry James' beat, whatever else one many think of it. It was not the America
he disliked; it was not the "down-town" of which he pro-
fessed to know himself ignorant. And if my great-aunt
was not precisely the America he approved, if, indeed,
with her perennial activity she at length became not
wholly unlike the rather over-shined and over-diamonded
type he disliked, there remains still my maternal grandmother, Mary Easton, who while not placeable in any
James' novel, retained always somewhat the atmosphere
of the plainer and early James, notably as in "Washington Square," and came certainly of the order of things
cognizable in James' New England figures; and my uncle
(great-uncle, to be exact) Amos Easton, who had bulged
out of his original mil huit cent trente into something
fairly identifiable with the jocular "parties" in James'

"Small Boy and Others." "The Thirties" would have arrived possibly eighteen years late in America.

Mary Easton was a confirmed romantic; she began to
read me Scott's novels in the seventh year of my age; she
conserved more illusions—if, indeed, romanticism be an
illusion! I give it up. She was "a monument of good sense"
à la New England, exceeded therein only by her cousin
Susannah. I suppose Scott himself was a "monument."
Her mind may have been like his, minus the narrative
urge, and tempered by romantic timidity befitting the
feminine nature of a now somewhat legendary era. Her
timidity was as egregious as it was unaffected. For instance, when the cowboys shot up the town of Spokane
—but I anticipate.

My "Uncle" Amos had retired from the "feed business,"
and from business in general, prematurely. He had built
a "place" at Tarrytown on the Hudson, in the intention
of being a country gentleman and of fostering fine art.
He acquired a set of ivory chess-men in lieu of a picture
which some artist found himself unable to paint, but for
which Amos had paid. He Amos collected a curious band
of dependents who ultimately helped to run his hotel.
One of them resembled Rosa Bonheur; she pursued a
career of masterly inactivity until the age of 87; never
wholly parasitic, she made small and neat sketches in
lead pencil, and was intermittently employed on "ac-
counts." Some other Easton imported the enthusiasm of
Viollet-le-Duc and "built" (presumably as architect) the
Castle, which, as many another ambitious domicile of the
period, has since been "turned into" a school.

The most adhesive of Uncle Amos' dependents was
Mary Pinker. As housekeeper she remained till his end,
whereupon she went into deep mourning: she desired
to wear a veil. This luxury of grief was denied her, and
this inhibition so injured her finer feelings that in the ensuing complications she suspended immediate contact
with the family, appearing only on more formal occa-

sions. She was, however, present at my great-aunt's third wedding—a Rubens-Tiepolo sort of affair. I know, for she sat in front of me. I had dodged familial enclave and was sitting in a less prominent pew with Mr. Bohun, a tall gaunt "Andy Jackson" type who had been something in oil and made terms with "The Standard" (Oil Co.) "soon enough."

When the sacrament had been pronounced Mary Pinker turned in her pew and said: "Oh, Mr. Bohun, it does so remind me of poor, dear Mr. Easton's funeral!" Mr. Bohun said: "Shut up, Mary Pinker!" She was crapey and very narrow of beam. All of which does not help the reader to grasp what Rip Weight was "up against" when he first struck New York City. Merely it is difficult for me to visualise the family of the Eastons without imagining Mary Pinker, shrivelled and swathed, and Clementia Eulalia Horne (Rosa Bonheur) and certain additional but less constant female figures in attendance. They would have been younger, possibly, in the late 'seventies, and earliest possible 'eighties, but in their cases it couldn't have, possibly!, mattered, or shown to the naked eye.

There remained Haddon Easton, invisible, and Maria Easton, Hermione's mother. When I say that Haddon Easton remained, the verb may be taken in all of its senses; he was at last report still remaining, invisible. A Sixth Avenue barber once asked me if I had seen him. For the first twenty years of my life I was led to suppose Haddon deceased. It is not suggested that he had "done anything," but rather a sort of persistence in various forms of re-action rather connected, in the familial mind, with his "having ideas." "He always had plenty of ideas." He did not, for example, continue to support Mary; he had put "Hermy" in a convent school for a few months, and refrained from paying the bills; he had, as definite manifestation of kinetic potentialities, "punched Amos' head," when the stubbier and more industrious brother had, on the front porch of the country gentleman's place in Tarrytown, declined finally and conclusively to lend Haddon any more money: and he had remained in, or retained an interest in "the business." If Amos saw him occasionally, the rest of the family did not. Mary Easton earned her own living, and Miss Hermy gradually became part of the family, i.e., the group unanym having its centre in Amos or in Amos' wife, as the observer chose to regard it.

Two groups of things must be gathered: firstly, that Rip was from Wisconsin: that Maria Easton had "other ideas about" Hermy: and that Rip's overcoat, though of very durable material and capable of resisting a great deal of weather, was neither of a cut nor of a timbre and colour combination that was then being, or had, so far as research can discover, ever been worn in New York.

Secondly, Maria Easton did not "really" approve of Aunt Hebe (pronounce "Heeb," not that the Eastons were ignorant of the correct pronunciation of Hebe, but for expedition's sake and compactness). Maria Easton was a Westover: we admit that her father's name was Almeny, and that her brothers were all three called Almeny, or rather so addressed on their envelopes. Maria admitted no lex Salica. She had small opinion of Almenys dead or living. She referred to her brothers, of whom she was fond, by isolated prænomena; she remembered that her mother had been a Westover at birth. She was indeed the Westover's cousin Maria, and so remained till her death, recognising a Bealdon connection in New York, where the Westovers had not manifestly remained.

Rip was from "The West," where, as he once told a member of not one of the oldest, but of *the* oldest Philadelphia families, not merely a Snowden, but a Lowden (pronounced Leoden)—Snowden that a man was lucky to know his own father. It will perhaps help to date the repartee, as it was then called, if we note that Euripides had used the adjective lucky without modern intensive qualification, though in male company at the time.

5

CHAPTER the Fifth: wherein are found certain digressions, chiefly because of a question asked me by an Englishwoman about whom there could have been no doubts whatsoever. It was at the time when I was regarded as a sort of calamaretti, to be sampled by the daring experimentalist—and to press the parallel and also to enlighten the reader—we may say that the Venetian octopus is delicious if caught young enough; later the flavour remains but the substance is slightly gristly and more difficult to be swallowed. She said to me: I read books about America, but what I can't make out is: Are they ladies and gentlemen like we are? (The "we" being purely racial and Anglican.) A full answer to this question might take a man the rest of his life. There is, however, the America of *la vieille roche*, and to say of an Englishman that he might be taken for a representative of this diminishing and almost legendary America, is as high a compliment as one can pay him.[1]

There is also a larger and heteroclite mass of American males who might be taken or mistaken for Englishmen, but their quality depends rather upon the kind of Englishman for whom they might be mistaken. Imitations of both class *a* and class *b* are perhaps more numerous than either, though there *is* a point at which the English cease altogether to be cynosure. For example the "god's own" type is not copied (i.e., in America; it may still have some vogue in the Dominions).

All of which things might be passed over, perhaps, were they not the very things which we most fail to know regarding any strange land or epoch. Gentlemen, fine gentlemen, *galantuomo*, perfect, nature's, also man, Man (as before the advent of the ten-cent magazine); as after

[1] I can not recall an occurrence *de facto*.

that advent, and, still later, after the grandiose concept of the cinema, Bull-moose, etc., all containing various crypto-grams each as complicated as any enigma of chivalry; some regarding the heart and some the cut of the waist-coat. *"O poca digna nobiltà di sangue."*

It cannot, according to Dante, be settled wholly upon factors of heredity, and the manners that "makyth" a man in one time or place would certainly unmake him in other. In the "Flamenca" the errant hero finds the great lord of the castle sitting in the great hall of the castle with his shirt off, and his wife's handmaids are scratch-ing his back, and he was a great lord and presumably "advanced" for the thirteenth century, for the next few hundred lines of the poem (what are a hundred lines to a writer of chivalry?) are devoted to exposition of the castle's annual laundering and bathing foray; with all available great kettles, go they to heat water by the river bank. And centuries later the Spanish ambassador at Naples spits in his servant's face as a compliment to his hostess, saying that everything else in her audience room is much too precious to receive his base mucus secretion. This is the renaissance when people were thinking of manners; I dare say they have thought of them in ages and stations of chaos, and that Castiglione's "Corteg-giano" was needed just as little books on etiquette have been needed, and as complete "Letter Writers" have been welcome.

At Montignac last year I found the complete guide for respectable bourgeois families. Anyone entering the bour-geoisie from below might for six francs be spared errors in everything from the *layette* to the funeral, with pleas-ures for mixed gatherings by the way.

In the time of Louis XVI, a lady of Goldoni's acquaint-ance spent her time solving the weekly "Engimas" in the then "Mercure de France"; she arose at night to write the solution of a rebus to her circle.

True, Voltaire does not, so far as I know, record similar activities in *his* circle, but he was out of Paris at the time.

A writer on "Caporetto" attributes the loss of the battle to Italy's lack of bourgeoisie from which officers can be made; in England three years ago one saw England nobly responding to the need for 300,000 new gentlemen. Marvellous resource of the nation! And in the arcades of the Piazza S. Marco one recognises the advantages of an accepted norm of appearance; or at least one wishes they wouldn't try to be English gentlemen.

And at the same time the most sensible thing Rip Weight ever did was to descend from the train for West Point, where he would have acquired an irreproachable uniform, immaculate "white ducks" and a rigid complete set of values.

Values, like clothing, can be obtained ready-made, and, incontrovertibly, ready-made suits do sometimes fit a figure: and if a man finds ready-made clothing that fits him better than what is known in America as "made to order," there seems to be only prejudice to prohibit his exploitation of the circumstances. And, incontrovertibly also, vast hordes of the genus gentleman would seem to have acquired their mental furnishing on the "ready-made" system, all of which does not answer the opening enquiry of this chapter: "ladies and gentlemen like we are?"

In mind? no. In manner? not precisely, yet sometimes yes. In clothing? if need be. A complete Herodotus would here diverge into a chapter on "The Dude," on the sufferings of a small but resolute band who determined to wear high hats in the smaller communities; on something that was even in my time called a "Prince Albert coat." After the Dude came the "Stiff" (word has a different connotation in Johannesburg: a Johannesburg "stiff" is in American a *bum* or *hoboe*). The American "stiff" was a person whose manners were rather like those of English permanent department officials.

Then came the democratisation of evening dress; the ready-made clothing companies flooding the magazines with male fashion plates, and all the recently (half generation) emigrants plunging into starched linen.

6

I have always been grateful to the Westovers for not taking passage on the "Mayflower"; they arrived decently upon the "Lion," before the rush and about three years after the Aldens.

I don't mean that they—the representative elder generation, Henry and Edward Westover, have referred to the matter in my presence; Maria Easton did that. Maria was, as the reader has forgotten, a Westover, there being no lex Salica in these matters.

In fraternal contrast it may be said that Henry Westover is a gentleman, distinctly American; that is to say he behaves like a rational creature, as, for instance, I should myself. Entering the drawing-room of his country house and finding the fire inadequate, Henry at once opened the porch-door, knowing where the logs were, had three of them on the fire in no time.

Edward, on the contrary, would have rung for a servant, or, if there had been no servant he would in any case have conveyed the impression of having rung for a servant, he would, in any case, have waited until something happened to cause an increased radiation of heat. There is, so far as I know, no symptom by which one can distinguish Edward from the impeccable norm accepted in England, save that possibly after long conversation one might notice a faint vowel modulation not very usual among the English. He would never have ventured the flat Eton collar.

Edward's sons are gentlemen in his wake. In the case of Henry's offspring I think possibly the first impression would be: This is an American businessman. One would discover on examination that he was, is, a gentleman. In the Edward family, both generations convey at first impact: Gentlemen; one continues the analysis from that point. Festus began his career with the determination to starve in New York, rather than be driven from the metropolis, and is a respected physician. Edward, from being a gentleman, has had great difficulty in discovering how to be anything else: he has somewhat drifted about the professions—in a charming manner; that must be insisted upon in the case of all of the Westovers.

Henry and Edward have been on the Exchange for so long that their seats are almost a patent of nobility. Further, to discriminate, it might be said that the talk at Henry's table ran to motor cars (when I knew it)—the family seemed to require several each—and to supplementary motor-boats and to the Exchange, merits of still and unstill market. I forget the exact term for the unquiet antithesis—it may possibly have been "jumpy."

Incidentally Henry had taken the Exchange seriously; he had "always said" his sons were not to follow him on to it, but they had seen to all that, and possibly to his old-fashioned modus of treating it. Henry had been solid, he was reputed to have "stood by" the family connections to such remote degree and so often that "one shouldn't really appeal." He even did me a turn once, who, being the grandson of a cousin, couldn't decently have been supposed to be in the running.

Edward had taken the Exchange as a bore and an imposition; it had bored him for forty years; he has, I presume, never had enough money; his ties were at one time said to have been the model of what the male New York cravat should be *in excelsis*. It is felt that conversation should include literature, limited; on the other hand there is the feeling that one should deal gently with the reputations of members of the family, especially if their endeavours have been recorded in Westminster Abbey. And so, perhaps, one should, unless one has a vigorous interest in the matter.

Which things being so, I found that, without any decision, without any sort of intention, I drifted more often to Edward's than to Henry's. Such the Westovers as I found them; what they were to "Rip" Weight in the early 'eighties must be left to conjecture. I doubt if he even "had" them as a separate impression, they would have arrived as an inexplicable and indirect influence in the formalities of Maria and of Hermy; Maria, of course, wanting Hermy to pair with someone who was prepared to live up to them, to live up possibly to the standard of Edward's neck-wear, if that were the period of its glory; or to the armorial bearings, and a work called "The Westover Family in America." Having drawn a dud in the conjugal struggle Maria may reasonably have exercised some anxiety about Hermy.

Such also is the snobbery (with, of course, all the Darwinian advantages) of the race, that all of us naturally cling to the greatest luxury we have known, at whatever period of our life it may overtake us. (Tragedy, as last year I heard it almost sobbed in a French village inn, "Et moi, j'étais patron; et maintenant suis ouvrier!"). Hermy had seen the Easton star at its zenith, with the Nyack place and her uncle's intention to be a country gentleman and a patron of the fine arts; she can't have liked the collapse, she can't have liked either the strain—if any— before the hotel was decided upon, or the early stages of its progress.

What one wants is the general touch equation: Maria feeling that Vera (Mrs. Edward) "went in for" society (conditioned by my own twenty years' later impression that the Edwards were perfectly simple people untroubled by this form of desire—though of course at

some anterior period . . . one could not absolutely have
sworn the contrary to have prevailed); plus the gentle
manner in which the Westovers remained graciously unconscious of Aunt "Heeb" in her later and encrusted
period; plus the then factor of my uncle Easton, who
certainly was not down-hearted. Even under the impact
of his brother's departing left-hander one felt that my
uncle Easton would have bounced, he would have hit the
porch floor, resumed the usual perpendicular posture
with an automatic and airy obesity; his straight little
mouth would, between his little cubical whiskers, have
resumed the accustomed crease of its smile. He, after
all, had always been comfortable; the first How (no
terminal *e*) had hung his scutcheon in Duxbury and told
his man to cook for his master and all and sundry; how
else could a person accustomed to leisure be expected to
maintain his wonted standard of victualling? Mr. Easton
must have given similar commands to his niggers. The
place was always darn'd comfortable. The folding beds
never snapped or decapitated or fell engulfing any visitor;
they devolved upon their own middles and had an extra
set of legs half way down.

"Rip" may have found it somewhat alarming, he presumably found Easton's chuckle and "haw" somewhat
alarming, this series of prodigious pop-guns of good humour: "An' I bet him a dollar an' the first thing I knew
in the morning was a fellah yelling hurrah for Grover,
and running off with my ash-barrel," plus bubbles and
gurgles of merriment.

Or possibly Rip's puzzlement was only that usual to
the long parallelogram object when confronted with the
stubbier, stockier form of humanity.

7

AT any rate, Rip retired to the fastnesses of the Saw-
Tooth Range, 5,000 ft. above sea-level (and five million

or thousand miles from ANYwhere, let alone from civilisation, New Yorkine or other), and conducted the opening negotiations in writing. He trusted the clerks' taste
at Tiffany's; he had in the interim found a new kind of
overcoat; he built what was then called the first plastered
house in Hailey. [Footnote: dwelling since enlarged, and
appearing in the local Press as "the residence now occupied by Mr. Plughoff."]

Before introducing the chief protagonists to this mining
town, i.e., one street lined with saloons (*anglicè:* pubs),
it may be well to introduce Mary Beaton. The historic
patronymic need cause no delay. The Washingtons, the
Calverts, the Entroughtys "who pronounce it Darby,"
and names from the History Plays belong now to persons
of colour. The Latin concept of the *familia* survived;
slaves had no patriarchal designation save in many cases
that of their masters. I have said that Uncle Amos' niggers
thought Miss Hermy "som'thin' spesh'l," just as in a minor
way their residue thought me something special, by
derivation—and among them Mary Beaton had been always "gaoin with Miss Hermy when she mahr'd" (as
later, indeed, Julia Crump always declared "Amh gaoin
tu cuuk fo' you, Marse Jo, when you get to de Whith
Hous' ")

[To attempt to convey the phonetics of the darker
American, with an Italian pen, and via a Cockney printer!
Icarus! Icarus!]

Mary Beaton was what has through two centuries of
English fiction been designated as a determined character: and if it was sporting of Hermy to attempt the
unknown, she had at least Rip's company and protection.
Mary Beaton was shipped on ahead, to the joy of the
local Press. Hailey, you will understand, had one hotel,
one street, 47 saloons, and one newspaper. Rip opened
the Govt. Land Office. Hailey had also one Nubian
citizen, barber: but Mary Beaton was new to them, likewise her raiment, which might, I suppose, be "conveyed"

to the English reader by saying that it ventured toward the "somewhat Teutonic," if this adjective may be held to differentiate between the public women of Cologne or Mainz, and those of Paris.

It must be borne in mind that in the opening of the war for secession the Southern States had probably a "right" to secede, if "right" were to be judged on written documents and on the spirit of the articles of Confederation which preceded the American Constitution. In course of this separatist dispute New York City had mooted secession from the State of New York, and negroes "hung from the lamp-posts" may have indicated an unwillingness to build black "freedom" on a structure of white slaughter. One of Kipling's characters has summarised the effects of the "War" ('60–65) as extermination of the Anglo-Saxon race in America in order that the Czeko-Slovaks might inherit Boston Common.

I know no "social documents" indicating quite the tonal status of New York negroes in the late 'fifties; nor yet any means of judging how many establishments were like that of my mother's Uncle Amos (before his crash) on which a plantation system tempered with wages of a sort had pertained. When my own memory dawns, a reasonable percentage of the negroes had "been there a long time"; some of them had been slaves " 'fo de woh," and there were enough older ones to leaven the lump and leave, I think, most of the "charm" alleged to have inhered in the patriarchal previous system.

The "race-problem" begins where personal friendliness ceases. "I ain't neveh haad no troeubl' wi'h niggarhs. Waz riz wi'h niggarhs. Ah mos' go dahn teh ma ambassy foh see de blak man at de do'h."

This feeling cannot be expected to obtain with families who have arrived in America since 1880, or who have met the black man as a competitor, or who find him insolent, precisely because having been accustomed to a courteous authority he will not put up with bad manners from low-browed Europeans. There are ninety different ways of saying "Damn nigger"; it requires knowledge to use the right ones.

Of course, one constantly hears: "The old ones, oh yes; but the *new* ones!!!" I cannot speak for the last dozen years. The nigger, like any other fine animal, is very quick to perceive certain tones of personality, of voice, modes of moving, not by cerebral analysis but by "feel." Some men never get on with horses; some men are perfect fools in the way they approach any animal.

If the old South had not been not only "destroyed," but if the actual old white population had not been so definitely, in such actual numbers, killed off and driven away, the "problem" might be in quieter state and "solutions" less in demand.

All of which is vain prologue to an attempt to convey Mary Beaton, the deep bosomed and affable, the "stylish" New York (City) negress of 1883, having been with Uncle Amos since the Flood, and always havin' been gaoin' with her Miss Hermy when she mahr'd;—or quite the equation of Mary Beaton—who, whatever else she may have been, was certainly the *product* of a very considerable civilisation—and Hailey, which was not; which, for the length of that one street bordered with wooden shacks, most of them selling, and one of them labelled, "Kentucky Hardware," simply was not.

Presumably some of the inhabitants had never seen anything as good as her clothes; as possibly none of the inhabitants had seen anything *like* them; styles travelled slowly in those days, in the lands north-west of the Mississippi; and whatever Mary Beaton had done to shed honour on the family had been done, we conjecture, with richness if not with Attic restraint. *Vera incessu!*

A galley under full sail and with oars; she was then of mature years, her progress was that of small, full-busted women who wish to look their full height, complicated by a hip-motion semblable to that supposed to be found among the danseuses of Andalusia. It was twenty-five years after this that she married the Reverend Mr. Hoban, by at least that number her junior—and is, I suppose, still a stylistic model to the members of his congregation.

In Hailey there was only the barber, and he her social inferior, somewhat *agreste*, at any rate unable to live up to her. Having put Rip's house (now occupied by Mr. Plughoff) in order, she had—while Rip and Hermy inspected Niagara Falls and paid a somewhat disappointing visit upon Thadeus—nothing to do but "sashay," and nowhere but the plank side-walk of Hailey whereon to perform her egress and ingress.

8

IT comes over me (it should probably come in parentheses) how much they must have talked politics. That Julia Crump should prognosticate official position is one thing, but that a child of six should lift up its miniature rockingchair and hurl it across the room in displeasure at the result of a national election can only have been due to something "in the air"; to some preoccupation of its elders, and *not* to its own personal and rational deductions regarding the chief magistracy of the Virgin Republic.

In this case it may have been that I was genuinely oppressed by the fear that my father would lose his job and that we should all be deprived of sustenance. It was in the days before "Civil Service," and an appalling percentage of Government employees were almost automatically "fired" as a "natural result" of every change in administration; fired after perhaps thirty years' service and with no prospects of a pension.[1]

[1] The Civil Services are still, I believe, unpensioned in the United States of America. (At date "Indiscretions" was written, 1920.)

Thadeus might have been expected to discuss the subject—I have no recollection of Thadeus, or of anything his save his beard—I am thinking of Uncle Amos, his lot. He was travelling in the South before the "war," and was caught there, presumably, by it; at any rate, there remain his permits to pass through the Rebel lines —but thirty years later, seeing that he never held office, that he never *did* anything political——! I give it up. I merely feel that in the years before I remember anything there must have been an infinite discussion of "Demys" and "G.O.P."

Amos and Mr. Fouquet can't have changed the subject, from the opening of the Easton until the years of their deaths. Note that Mr. Fouquet was old French Louisiana, and "red-hot Tammany," and that his bald head and drooping, double-length Bourbon or Chauncey Depew nose and white whiskers were separated from Uncle Amos' chubby, black-whiskered visage by only one place at table—that of Mrs. Fouquet, stiff, plump, encased in dull green with brown reflets, or dull brown with dull green reflets, and in either case a good deal of braid, and a perfectly non-committal, good-humoured, stiff little smile. And that Uncle Amos was solid Republican, and that for at least two meals every day for fifteen years there must have been an uninterrupted flow of facetious insult, and that they must have found it "essential," or at any rate the survivor must have found it essential, as he only survived seven months.

But it, the politics and the popularity, must have been the tone of some period or other, some period that read "Puck" and "Judge," and that is mirrored in the drawings and crude (? Rowlandson gone to the bad) colours of those back numbers. I don't mean that I actually remember seeing my Uncle Amos reading a copy of "Judge," or even in possession of same, or that Mr. Fouquet quoted the Tammany publication, but there must have been some aroma of the untempered "illustrated joke" about niggers

and hen-coops, and of the cartoons of the symbolic Elephant and Mule that was germane to their jocularity, the
shrill, high, normal tone of Fouquet, ascending to pure
Punch and Judy or drooping to a false double-bass (it is
just possible that this was done for my benefit and that
he did not use it in "ordinary conversation," but I doubt
this hypothesis. I adored both him and my great-uncle),
playing into Amos' fruity chuckle, and all about God
alone knows what, about Tammany, about Chauncey
Depew, or having to do with High Tariff.

But they all must have "talked politics," even old
Quackenbush, who looked like Napoleon III, and was,
presumably, put at the head of "the other long table"
because he lacked humour, or was too solemn to keep
his temper in facetious conversation.

I want merely to indicate a factor, both in what must
have been the tone of a gentleman, and in the milieu
from which Miss Hermione fled to the Saw Tooth, preceded by that serene and stately presence, Mary Beaton.

They always thought it ought to be "done"—i.e., that
someone should put "it" (Hailey and environs, and Mary
Beaton on the plank walk, and Blue-Dick and the rest
of the "characters") into "a story"—i.e., the form of
washed-out Maupassant with the "humour" and pathos
and nice feelings and bell in the last ¶, which the ten
American monthlies offered in lieu of literature. They, of
course, couldn't do it; it enriched their table talk for life,
but it couldn't be passed on to magazine writers . . .
"of course Owen Wister," etc. There were stories about
the West—what they had was aroma and anecdotes:
"Kentucky Hardware," for example, who called it that
because he didn't want "his folks home" to know what he
was doing; and the man who sawed wood one week and
when subsequently invited to repeat the operation (ten
days' interval), said: "Saaw wud? Saaaw WUD!! Say,
Rip, dew yew wanter gao East an' sell-a-mine, Rip? I got
ten-thousan'-in-the bank."

This fable indicates the mutability of fortune in new land where silver is digged from the earth. There was likewise the scenery, miles of it, miles of real estate, "most of it up on end"; Shoshone Falls "bigger than Niagara"— either upwards or sideways, but for some reason neglected by fashion.

Of course they didn't, couldn't "do anything with it"; in the first place they hadn't the "seein' eye," and in the second an anecdote, as the change in Hank Bains's fortunes, is merely the sort of thing that has occurred in cheap imaginative work since the beginning of time; the only possible interest inheres in its being the man who is sawing wood in *your* backyard at the moment, and not in Baghdad or Ispahan. It might become literature if one knew Hank's circumstantial or psychological vicissitudes before "gold was struck" on his claim, or melodrama if "Rip" had been a cruel oppressor or hated cinema "rival." Otherwise it remains an anecdote in one paragraph.

When I say they hadn't the "seein' eye" I mean that they never succeeded in conveying the visual appearance of any one of their characters as distinct from any other. There was an almost complete lack of detail. Horace Morgan the gambler wore a long black coat (? frock) down to his knees; Blue Dick may have owed the adjective to an accident with blasting powder; of Curley, Poison, and Mike Bennet, nothing remains but the indications of nomenclature; of the variations from cinema cow-boy "rig-out" (i.e., habiliment) to that of miner's clothing—apart from the fact that the miner in action carried sticks of dynamite in his boots—to the variants of presumably "wrong-fitting" store clothes one has but scantiest indication. There is a photograph of "Rip" at somewhat later period, presumably formal in intention, which shows him in a presumably expensive but very queerly cut "pair of pants," but their form may have been temporal and not exclusively regional, or at least the

factors may have blended . . . or simply, the tailor may
have calculated for the foot-wear.

9

HE (Dick) was most sympathetic after the "accident";
he sat up with Rip all night, and bored a hole through
his big toe nail to relieve the pressure, and told him
stories, told him how he loved his "dawg," faithful for
years, and then how he found him "co-old as a st-hone
and ded-as-a-macker'l."

It will be seen that if they, Rip and Hermy, hadn't the
seein' eye they had occasionally an ear for cadence, and
retained a line or two of the idiom.

Euripides appreciated Dick's delicacy in not having
shot him. The idea that life is a burden and the desire
to enter into the eternal placidity of non-being were not
in Rip's mental outfit; he understood that Dick had loved
his lost "dawg," that Dick had the finest possible feelings,
but that accidents in mines were unavoidable and that
the next one would be somewhat worse; also as he could
not walk and as his "cayoos" could not carry him about
the mine, he mounted that animal, Hermy likewise
mounting hers, and the jeune ménage retired to the legal
centre. I have never understood quite how much of the
"law" was under Rip's supervision; needless to say he
was not in the executive branch; he had "opened the
Government Land Office" and "miners came in from 200
miles to file their claims." This was because Thadeus,
who opposed nepotism, had "been through" and bought
a brace of mines, and Idaho being then a territory there
were no senators, and probably no one but Thadeus and
a few of the railroad pioneers had heard of the place, so
that it was quite easy to get Rip appointed—especially
as there may have been quite a number of young men
who would not have cared to go so far, for a very indefinite "prospect": also it was not nepotism, it was not

for Rip's convenience but for that of Thadeus, who by getting Rip a Government job got also, gratis, a perfectly honest representative to keep his eye on the property.

Hence the first plastered house; hence the ingress of Mary Beaton; hence Hermy's perception that it ought to go into a story—the main street where the minister's salary was collected over the bars (one elder took one side of the street and the other the other), the décor of weather boards, topless mountains, Horace Morgan's black coat and felt hat, rapid permutation of fortunes, gents dying "with their boots on": which was too much for Mary Beaton, unsustained by romance and a sense of how it would look in Harper's Magazine. She couldn't bear to say good-bye to "Miss Hermy": she left at midnight, without her variegated assortment of clothing, and was duly "blown up" by Aunt Heeb. Hermy's next "maid," *anglicè* "general," married a rich prospector and went to live at the hotel.

Rip drank a certain amount of lemonade at the various saloons in the main street, without giving offence. How he did so must remain his own secret. He did not carry a gun; he had bought one, but his cousin, Harve, took it away saying he'd "Better not 'cause it might go off and hurt someone." He borrowed one once to go up to the mine, but there was no call for it: he tried five shots at an impassive rabbit, and retained one for the return journey. "After he finished his lunch at the top of a divide, he looked down back along the road and saw a mountain lion sniffing at the paper he'd had his lunch in." On considering the ratio of five bullets to one rabbit, and his remaining cartridge, he "put for" the nearest habitation. Hermione has always regretted that lion skin.

Hermione was taken out into the mountains and it was like the dawn of creation. Hermione went to live at the hotel and some of the guests objected to the hotel servants dancing in the ballroom after dinner. The prospector and his wife were also staying at the hotel. The prospector's wife declined to join in the protest saying, "I really couldn't quite; you know I was Mrs. Weight's maid before I married."

Kerosene was a dollar a gallon. Oysters came in a can. Mary Beaton was still in disgrace; it was months before Aunt Heeb readmitted her to the gleaming respectabilities of her service. Hailey stole the Court House: Ketchum collared the Terminus of the railway.

To understand *that particular* visit to the mines it is necessary to know that according to the then laws of mine-claiming one was allowed a certain amount of mining land free. The Government permitted you to "stake out" so many acres on condition that you worked it; that you took from it each year gold worth a certain amount; if you failed to do this, anyone else wanting a mine could "jump" your claim, i.e., include it entire, or any part of it he chose in his own claim.

Dick, Curley and Co. were hired by Thadeus to perform these formalities; but seeing that their own personal ownership had advantages they decided to omit a few details. Or rather they dug a certain number of tons of rock which did not contain the ore, and excused themselves by saying that the vein was played out; that the mine couldn't be worked to profit.

Rip, who in some unexplainable period had acquired the knowledge of metals, went up to prove that it could. By the time the boulder collided with him, he had already the proofs in his various bags and pockets.

This, however, did no one any good, as it took the Courts 18 years to assert the fact; and in any case it probably would have benefited no one but Thadeus, so that, like many another unrelated kinesis, its significance must lie chiefly in the realm of pure knowledge.

And the mountain rats were as big as cats, and to hear them in the camp kitchen you would think they took down each pan and banged it.

And Rip went into the mine and then Hermy could see

him come out at another opening a thousand feet higher up; and they said: "Weight has lungs like a bellows."

And everything was uncorrelated, and nothing bore particularly on anything else. And an Englishman came out to look after some mines that a company had bought, and he was shocked that all the men in the mines got the same pay (dols per diem) whether they were skilled blasters, or whether they just pushed the trucks up to the mine-mouth. And he tried to adjust the matter according to his own ideas, and one night he got on his horse and got over the county line . . . . about as fast as the horse would agree to. (He didn't treat. He just went into a saloon and ordered his drink and drank it and went out again.)

10

BEFORE the birth of the infant Gargantua, the great elephant Sampson broke loose from the travelling circus, and upset the lion cages and chased his keeper out of the tent; and his keeper jumped on his cayoos and put for the railroad siding, and you could have seen the cowboys out after it, letting off their six-shooters into its rear.

I heard it all from Rip twenty times over, before the trainer wrote his reminiscences (illustrated, "Saturday Evening Post"). The trainer omits the detail of the cowboys, his attention having been fixed on the narrow opening between the two ore cars, because an elephant "never goes round anything." It was undoubtedly very clever of the trainer to get the mad animal wedged in between the angle of those cars where it could be dealt with. And they tied down the elephant Sampson and beat him with hot iron bars, and he grit "on them with his teeth," and they couldn't make him trumpet. And his keeper begged them not to kill him, but they had to anyhow, only a few months later.

And as the inhabitants weren't uncontaminated savages and as Fraser's "Golden Bough" was not in their list of reading, they none of them realised what it meant. ("Il vero intendimento," as Dante remarks, of the first sonnet he sent to Guido.)

And the infant Gargantua was born, and was photographed, and Maria Easton came out to see if he looked like his pictures. And the cowboys, as we have written, shot up the town of Cheyenne, where she had to change cars and spend the night. Forty of 'em came down the main street on their ponies, yelling and letting off their six-shooters. Of course they didn't do any harm.

Only it must be remembered that Maria Easton had been known to turn a corner and wring a strange door-bell for protection, because she thought *a man* was following her in the street. And she didn't understand what it meant. It might have, to her disordered mind, signified Fenimore Cooper Indians scalping all the inhabitants. And the hotel had only wooden partitions, and you could hear everything that went on in the next room. And there wasn't any lock on her door.

["Lock! Lock!" as Rip said to me fifteen years later. "You wouldn't, a man wouldn't, lock his door out there. If you had locked your door, they'd suspicion you."]

And Maria Easton got on the train next morning and came to Hailey, and she said, "Oh! Rip, how could you bring my daughter to *such* a place?"

And Rip felt somewhat flabbergasted.

Then they had a Chinaman to do the cooking and he was a model of virtue. Anything he was shown how to do, that did he exactly in replica, until when there was an "important dinner" with company, he failed to distinguish between the implement for removing crumbs from the table (implement known in those days as a crumb-brush, an often long, curved implement, about the sixth part of a circle's circumference, with bristles on the under-side) and the hearthbrush; and with ceremony and gravity he removed the crumbs with the hearthbrush; and the company maintained its decorum until he had retired. But from the kitchen he heard their hysteria, and there was a great noise in the kitchen "and you would have thought he was breaking all the dishes" altogether; and after a long and anxious interval the dessert "finally came in."

Then Hermy went to the hotel, whither the prospector's wife had preceded her; because there was only one hotel and no more cook-housemaids whatsoever.

And Hermy always thought it was very nice of the prospector's wife not to sign the protest about the hotel-servants using the ballroom.

And Hermy couldn't stand the high altitude any longer, and had to be taken back east in the blizzard, behind the First Rotary Snow-plough. And the infant Gargantua had the croup, and woke all the people in the "sleeper." And the inventor of the First Rotary Snow-plough was on board, and he said, "Madame, if you will give that child a little kerosene oil it will cure it." And Hermy was indignant. And Gargantua barked for an hour longer; and no one got any sleep in the sleeper. And the inventor of the First Rotary Snow-plough said again to Hermione: "Madame, I have reared seven myself, and they have all had croup. And I have cured all their croups with a few drops of kerosene oil, dripped onto a lump of sugar."

And Hermione, at last, consented; and the Infant Gargantua slumbered until the train pulled into Chicago.

Thus was the Infant Gargantua saved from a severe attack of the croup.

And as Joel the brother of his great-grandfather rode on the first railroad train in America, so the Infant Gargantua rode behind the First Rotary Snow-plough.

"Et celuy temps passa comme les petits enfans du pays c'est assavoir: à boire, manger et dormir . . . . Tousjours se vaultroit par les fanges, se mascaroit le nez . . . il se mouschoit à ses manches . . . patronilloit par tout lieu . . . beuvoit en mangeant sa soupe, mangeoit sa fouace sans pan, pissoit contre le soleil, s'asséoit entre deux selles le cul à terre, etc., et gardoit la lune des loups."

11

AND the infant Gargantua lay in his perambulator or baby-carriage (*anglicè:* pram) in the back-yard (*anglicè:* garden) of 24 E. 47th St., by the cellar doorway, and above the cellar was the basement, and above the basement was the first floor. And at the window of the back parlour Amos Easton bulged from a small stubby comfortable red plush easy-chair; and he tied the end of his wife's 20 sewing cotton to the stem of large crimson strawberry and lowered it toward Gargantua.

And this was to teach the infant Gargantua to look about; to look "up" and to be ready for the benefits of the gods, whether so whither they might come upon him. And when he had devoured the strawberry, the No. 20 best sewing cotton was drawn up, and another berry descended.

And at the end of the street jingled the small horse bells of the Madison Avenue horse-cars, bobbing down toward the white-washed tunnel, and beyond the car line was the Express Company, and beyond that the tracks from the "Grand Central," invisible because of the wall and the Express Company; and beyond that was 596, Lexington Avenue—with the cable cars.

And the infant Gargantua spoke the English tongue and used syntax and eschewed the muliebria of diminutives. And at the age of two years, less two months, he gave a correct medical diagnosis of his ailments, to the great amazement of old Dr. Dowling, who had expected him to say "Goo-ah" in response to his (Dowling's) enquiries.

And at the age of two years and four months he denounced Mary Beaton (in error) for wasting his talcum, when she spilt the baking-powder for the biscuits (*anglicè:* scones.)

And at the age of two years and five months he said: "Ma Easton is a steer." Indeed, both he and his praeprogenetrix had in their manners something of that definition which Dante adumbrates in his "e come quel che altra cura stringea," or the "vuolse cosi colà," some implication that their acts and tendencies rested upon the primal necessities of *anangke,* and his adjudgment was in this case presumably due to collision.

And at the age of two years and six months he was taken to Newport for the spring season, and at the age of three years he was taken to the Farm with the mansard slate roof with a cast-iron railing lifting its stiff dentelation about it, where dwelt his great-grandfather Ezekiel, with Joel (*his* brother) and Thadeus, the grandfather of Gargantua. And whither came Maria, mother of Hermione, and Albert, the uncle of Euripides. And Gargantua walked in the footsteps of his great-grandfather Ezekiel, and he made for himself a cane and leant heavily upon it in walking, in the manner of his great-grandfather Ezekiel, and he spent as much time as possible in the large double kennel of the sheepdogs.

And the serpent appeared early in his garden: Venus in Sagittarius blazing near the midheaven.

As a record of contemporary manners, only dubious value can attach to a period when one's powers of observation, such as they were, would seem to have exhausted their results in the kinesis of mimicry and to have left but the scantiest subjective record, and of which period there seems to be no spoken tradition, save that Albert preferred the Episcopal (Church of England) faith because "it interfered neither with a man's politics nor his religion," and that when (quite apart from any theological technicality) the inhabitants of Chippewa Falls being of one but wholly inactive mind, so that the

Methodist minister and his family were without sufficient provisions, he had driven the farm wagon from door to door, until gathering comestibles, and delivering same to the parson, he had added the cogent suggestion that he should now "get out and earn an honest living." Hermione found him amusing. I retain a vague approbation, possibly ex post facto and contracted from Hermione. Joel also I approved, holding in somewhat lower esteem my direct antecedents of their respective generations.

It was perhaps natural that Thadeus should have seen the grandiose possibilities of farming in Wisconsin, without greatly considering the effect of 40 and even 60 degrees below the zero Fahrenheit upon the ultimate products of the soil, and perhaps typical of the religious genius of the American people that in the year of our Lord 1888 there should have been a widely disseminated belief that cattle were in some mysterious way "better" for having their horns clipped; and equally typical of the wonder-working primordial *Monos* that Rip should be left to deal with sixty sore-horned cows and a firm disinclination on the part of farm hands to milk or to "monkey with" the females of the genus *bos* in that condition. And it was, in similar, natural that Thadeus should have landed Rip in said circumstances with no very definite understanding as to what Rip should get out of it, beyond the use of mansarded refuge (or rather such parts as were not given over to tribal elders), and some portion of the produce of the chill soil, and of course the vast "possibilities."

Rip has never been able to give me a coherent explanation of *why* people thought cows were "better" with their horns cut off; but neither for the matter of that is he able to explain why or how he knows the exact fineness of silver by squinting through a glass bottle. The bottle contains "silver solution" and one drops in N4Xq or something of that sort and observes a commotivity of the atoms, after which one writes 987 or 979 or 991, or possibly it is 897, 917, 884 on a blackboard and picks up the next cylindrical and vitreous encasement of liquid.

I am by no means surprised that Rip should have forsaken the vast possibilities of Wisconsin for the bare but more regular emoluments of the Treasury service. This does not mean that Rip is, from the years 1889 to the present, to be envisaged as a stately or even rigid figure bearing a chapeau *haute forme* and a good deal of manner, as specified in His Majesty's regulations. I can with difficulty convey, I shall be perhaps wholly unable to convey, the degree in which it does not mean any of the objective attributes of similar English situation. I record merely that upon Rip's first visit to Europe he visited His Majesty's Mint, and that His Majesty's Mint seemed perhaps a little surprised. They had, perhaps, not had a visitor; they may, for any objective affirmation to the contrary, have been prey to some vague predisposition that they themselves were about to *"be* had." Simply there was Rip, perfectly amiable, soft hat, some sort of Government credentials; there was also a lanky whey-faced youth of 16, presence unexplained save by consanguinity.

We did not on that occasion burrow into the vitals of the institution. We did not "saunter" and dodge about among stamping presses, or try our strength on apparently trifling but utterly unliftable sacks of gold coin. There was none of that genial "You can have it if you will carry it out," with which the, I think, 10,000 dol. size bag used to be treated. Or it may have been possibly the 10,000 dols. which one could just lift and the 20,000 dols. which was so amiably and unavailingly offered one by its guardians.

The individual assigned to our reception in the highly English institution seemed mainly concerned with his own lofty demeanour or bearing and but vaguely implicated in the refinement, testing and coining of metals. He was there through no fault of his own, or at least seemed to beg you (from an altitude) to consider that however suspicious his own presence there might be, it was nothing, oh! abysmally nothing, in comparison with the suspectibility of your own. Natural selection has endowed perhaps the British official with another, a second pair of eyebrows, not perhaps visible in the first sense, but like the spectral planets discernible in their way, and raised, seeking a precedent, possibly, in an upper and rarefied air.

And yet after 18 years of reflection and a certain number of cosmopolitan contacts, I am still unable to see that that chap "had anything" "on" my progenitor—which does not in the least mean to say that I would not rather deal with six British Officials in any formal matter—say, passports, or something of that sort—than be subjected to one encounter with equivalent representatives of my own natal Republic.

12

I have perhaps adumbrated too dark a national bearing in the foregoing antithesis, which may have been but that of two individual personalities. Of the "old" Philadelphia Mint I remember the Greek "temple" facade, if not "in," at any rate indebted to the taste that built Monticello; the taste of the only American President who ever wanted a gardener who could play the french horn and take his place in a quattuor of an evening; one of perhaps half-a-dozen Presidents with whom one would have cared to hold a second or third conversation.

It is contendable that the national taste in Presidents has declined, keeping pace with progress, as exemplified (in parenthesis) by the Bohuns. Old man Bohun was not only a gentleman but the fine old type. And his son is a stockbroker, roaring himself hoarse every day in the Wheat Pit, and using the word gentlemen (which his father did seldom or never) very freely in the necessary committee work at the golf club.

And this dissolution is taking place in hundreds of American families who have not thought of it as a decadence and may, reasonably, be mirrored in the national modus and institutions.

So that if the old Mint didn't exactly show the results of Jefferson's inquiries for the exact proportions of La Maison Carrée of Nîmes, it at any rate had a moderate number of sensible columns, and a reposeful chunky appearance, befitting the deity of coinage rather than the harpies of fluctuation.

In the rotunda one found various derelicts of the G.A.R., sitting in wooden arm-chairs, with some obsolete weapons in the vicinity. These poor old bulwarks of the Union were, I believe, generally shaken up when the "Demys" came into office. At other times they must have run through considerable small talk and consumed a fair deal of chewing tobacco (as, say, from the years 1865–95).

They had in earlier instance clustered about an old five-barrelled howitzer, but in the time of my more vivid recollection this lethal antiquity no longer menaced the Chestnut Street portal. A peaceful, I think, cylindrical steam radiator had, to the best of my memory, taken its place, and the rifles with fixed bayonets were no longer carried by the guard.

The infant Gargantua saluted these veterans and stodged up the stairs to the right, avoiding, that is, the "cabinet" or room where the coin collection was kept, avoiding likewise the bowels of the institution. Rip would be standing by a highish shelf-table before a window, and part of the window obscured by a black-board divided into small squares. He would squint through the remaining cylindrical bottles seriatim, and write the due proportion of thousandths in the square assigned to the bottle.

Or he would perhaps be seated at a roller-top yellow desk containing 23 drawers, 47 slides and cubby-holes, numerous private possessions of Rip's, stray lumps of Govt. gold, strips, filaments, blank coin discs, photos of Hermione, official pencils, religious and other periodicals, samples of ore sent in by hopeful aspirants to fortune (chiefly iron pyrites), clippings from "gold-bricks," which still had a regular sale in those days, and with which the purchasers invariably came to that spot and received with varying degrees of equanimity and melodrama the news that a brick to be valuable must be gold all the way through, or that a brick well known to its maker may easily be bored or clipped in such a manner that the clipping or boring will be of a substance not very widely distributed throughout the main mass of the object.

On the other side of the large cubical room the infant Gargantua beheld the back of Abe Bickersteth. This was the part of Bickersteth most commonly exposed to humanity. Bickersteth had been in the Mint personally or in the persons of his progenitors ever since there had been any Mint to be in; before, in fact, as a Bickersteth had made the first one, from which the present chunky edifice had expanded.

Bickersteth turned in his chair and regarded Gargantua with a benign and courteous disapproval. As he had never communicated with the outer world it is impossible to discover whether he was *really* widowed, whether he was bound to the wheel of his mysteries, mourning consciously or otherwise that three husky Bickersteths would all of them prefer large civil engineering salaries at thirty to the prospect of 3,000 dols. per annum after his death, and Rip's death, and the death of any of the surviving "boys" in the office who might reasonably have expected the "step up."

Whatever Bickersteth thought was, remained, and remains, unknown to Rip and to the boys in the office, Bickersteth was the chief of that office. There is no recorded instance of his having commented upon any procedure of that day, or of any day previous or succeeding. I do not know that any subordinate ever committed an error, but I am convinced that if Abe Bickersteth had ever discovered an error he would have made a small sort of hook or "v" in lead pencil and the "v" would have been about twice as long on the right side as the left, or else he would have refrained from making that "v," and in either case he would have presented his back to the delinquent and gone toward some other part of the workings slightly distrait and inscrutable.

The infant Gargantua went across the hall into the office where most of the gold balances were, where the boys were, where Rip had been until old Mr. McIlveigh had kindly consented to "pass on." Gargantua entered. Flynn gave him a nickel. He carried it back in triumph to Rip and Hermione, who looked horrified. She said acquisitiveness was not in his province and that he had better return it. Had he thanked Mr. Flynn? In any case he must return it.

He had not thanked Mr. Flynn. He returned it reluctantly, and with verbatim rendering of Hermione on the proper relation between himself and coins current. When he got to the word "mercenary" or some such Hermionesque polysyllable Mr. Flynn looked a little surprised. He may even have said "Come again!" which is an American expression meaning "Sir, I perhaps, or perhaps do not, quite grasp your verbal intention."

Hermione had somewhat that effect on the boys.

The principle of gold assaying can be grasped by the normal mind. You weigh a sample of metal, you then place it on a cupel of something looking like chalk; this is placed in an incredibly fiery furnace, and at a certain degree of fieryness the base elements are consumed or mopped up by the cupel. You then weigh the brilliant residue, and with certain repetitions, precisions, precautions, you know the fineness of the metallic mass.

Any fool might do it with infinite patience; it cannot be done with postal scales; the gold balance lives in its own glass house; the gold and the weights are lifted by longish forceps. The balances have tantrums in thundery weather. They will weigh you an eyelash; they will weigh you a bit of hair an eyelash long, but which weighs considerably less than an eyelash.

I have known Rip to weigh a man's name on his visiting card. Very simple. You weigh the card, then you have the man write his name on it in pencil; then you weigh the card with the signature. This is, however, rather a stunt.

For silver, as I have said, you just look at some stuff in a bottle. That's all, just as an art critic looks at a picture, and says, "No, not a Rembrandt," eh—eh; and, on consideration, not a Hals, either.

POSTSCRIPT

As an experiment it needs no justification, but to reprint it? Re? Because it is rather unavailable; and to print it in the first place? There is a gap—between, that is, the place the Great H. J. leaves off in his "Middle Years" and the place where the younger writers try to start some sort of faithful record. One offers one's little contribution to knowledge, and one stops (A), because there is something else one wants, more intensely, to do, and (B) because there are prosateurs ready to do this sort of record with more vigour and enthusiasm, and probably with more interest in prose than one has oneself.

At any rate my title fits the whole series, to which my fragment is (without any of the succeeding authors being in the least to blame) a sort of foreword. They have set out from five very different points to tell the truth about *moeurs contemporaines,* without fake, melodrama, conventional ending. The other MSS. are considerably more interesting than is this one of mine, which couldn't have come anywhere else in the series, and which, yet, may have some sort of relation to the series, and even a function, if only as a foil to Bill Williams' *The Great American Novel.*   —1923

The last paragraph applied to the whole "Inquest" series, six volumes indicating the state of prose after *Ulysses,* or the possibility of a return to normal writing. The six volumes were:

Indiscretions

Women and Men, by F. M. Ford

The Great American Novel, by W. C. Williams

England, by B. M. G. Adams

Windeler's Elimus, and

the short prose pieces by Hemingway, since included in his "In Our Time."

The series constituted a critical act.

IMAGINARY LETTERS

IMAGINARY LETTERS[1]

1. WALTER VILLERANT TO MRS BLAND BURN

My dear Lydia,

Your rather irascible husband asks for "Aunt Sallys"; with the Pyrénées before me and at this late date, it is difficult to provide them. I agree with at least half he says. I am, with qualifications, Malthusian. I should consent to breed under pressure, if I were convinced in any way of the reasonableness of reproducing the species. But my nerves and the nerves of any woman I could live with three months, would produce only a victim—beautiful perhaps, but a victim; expiring of aromatic pain from the jasmine, lacking in impulse, a mere bundle of discriminations. If I were wealthy I might subsidize a stud of young peasants, or a tribal group in Tahiti. At present *"valga mas estar soltero"*, I will not take Miss J. nor her income, nor the female disciple of John.

There is no truce between art and the public. The public celebrates its eucharists with dead bodies. Its writers aspire to equal the oyster: to get themselves swallowed alive. They encompass it.

Art that sells on production is bad art, essentially. It is art that is made to demand. It suits the public. The taste

[1] Wyndham Lewis had started a series of Imaginary Letters in *The Little Review* (1918), and was interrupted by his going into the army. E. P. continued the series.

of the public is bad. The taste of the public is always bad. It is bad because it is not an individual expression, but merely a mania for assent, a mania to be "in on it".

Even the botches of a good artist have some quality, some distinction, which prevents their pleasing mass-palates.

Good art weathers the ages because once in so often a man of intelligence commands the mass to adore it. His contemporaries call him a nuisance, their children follow his instructions, and include him in the curricula. I am not lifting my voice in protest, I am merely defining a process. I do not protest against the leaves falling in autumn.

The arts are kept up by a very few people; they always have been kept up, when kept up at all, by a very few people. A great art patron is a man who keeps up great artists. A good art patron is a man who keeps up good artists. His reputation is coterminous with the work he has patronized. He can not be an imbecile.

There are a few more people capable of knowing good art when they see it. Half of them are indifferent, three fourths of them are inactive, the exceeding few side with the artist; about all they can do is to feed him. Others, hating his art, may from family or humanitarian motives, feed and clothe him in spite of his art. . . . and attempt to divorce him from it.

These statements are simple, dull. One should write them in electric lights and hang them above Coney Island, and beside the Sarsaparilla sign on Broadway! The Biblical Text Society should embellish them upon busses.

Unfortunately the turmoil of Letts, Finns, Esthonians, Cravats, Niberians, Nubians, Algerians, sweeping along Eighth Avenue in the splendour of their vigorous un-washed animality will not help us. They are the America of to-morrow.

(The good Burn believes in America; the naive English, mad over apiculture, horticulture, arboriculture, herbiculture, agriculture, asparagiculture, etc., always believe in America. . . . until they have seen it.)

The turmoil of Finns, Letts, etc., is "full of promise", full of vitality. They are the sap of the nation, our heritors, the heritors of our ancient acquisitions. But our job is to turn out good art, that is to produce it, to make a tradition.

"My field must be ploughed, but the country has need of quiet" (La Famille Cardinal). "I admire Epicurus. He was not the dupe of analogies". Need I give references for all my quotations?

This nonsense about art for the many, for the majority. J'en ai marre. It may be fitting that men should enjoy equal "civic and political rights", these things are a matter of man's exterior acts, of exterior contacts. (Macchiavelli believed in democracy: it lay beyond his experience.) The arts have nothing to do with this. They are man's life within himself. The king's writ does not run there. The voice of the majority is powerless to make me enjoy, or disenjoy, the lines of Catullus. I dispense with a vote without inconvenience; Villon I would not dispense with.

Bales are written on the false assumption that you can treat the arts as if they were governed by civic analogies. The two things are not alike, and there is an end to the matter.

It is rubbish to say "art for the people lies behind us". The populace was paid to attend greek drama. It would have gone to cinemas instead, had cinemas then existed. Art begins with the artist. It goes first to the very few; and, next, to the few very idle. Even journalism and advertising can not reverse this law. I have scribbled a very long letter, and not answered half the good William's diatribe. My regards to Mrs Amelia.

Yours,
Walter Villerant

2. WALTER VILLERANT TO MRS BLAND BURN

My dear Lydia,

Russians! No. William is *matto* over his Russians. They are all in the beginning of *Fumée*—all the Russians. Turgenev has done it: a vaporous, circumambient ideologue, inefficient, fundamentally and katachrestically and unendingly futile set of barbarians. Old Goff says of savages: "I like savages. They do nothing that is of the least possible use, they do nothing of the least possible interest. They are bored. They have ceremonies. In the malice of boredom, the medicine man makes them dance in a ring for hours in order to *degust* their stupidity, *per assaggiarlo,* to bask in the spectacle of a vacuity worse than his own".

I mistrust this liking for Russians; having passed years in one barbarous country I can not be expected to take interest in another. All that is worth anything is the product of metropoles. Swill out these nationalist movements. Ireland is a suburb of Liverpool.

And Russia! The aged Findell comes back in ecstasy, saying: "It is just like America". That also bores me. They say Frankfort-am-Main is just like America.

Paris is not like America. London is not like America. Venice is not like America. Perugia is not like America. *They are not the least like each other.* No place where the dew of civilization has fallen is "just like" anywhere else. Verona and Pavia are different. Poitiers is different. Arles is a place to itself.

Dostoïevsky takes seven chapters to finish with an imbecile's worries about a boil on the end of his nose. Dostoïevsky is an eminent writer. Let us thank the gods he existed. I do not read Dostoïevsky. Several young writers have impressed me as men of genius, by reason of tricks and qualities borrowed from Dostoïevsky. And so on . . . .

I have also read Samuel Butler. And poetry? As the eminently cultured female, Elis writes me that her little cousin will have nothing to do with it. Rubbish! Her little
cousin will read Li Po, and listen to the rondels of Frois-
sart. I know, for I tried her.

Elis has imbibed a complete catalogue, with dates,
names of authors, chief works, "influence" of A.B.C. on
M.N.O. etc., etc. with biographies of the writers, and
"periods". Buncomb! Her cousin, who knows "nothing at
all", is ten times better educated. No? She "doesn't like
poetry". *Anglice:* she doesn't like Swinburne. It is not in
the least the same thing. And she is worried by most of
Dowson, etc.

Elis appeals to me as possessing "manner" or "prestige", i.e. professorial aspects, to coerce the rebellious infant.

She says I used to read Swinburne "so splendidly".
Damn it! I believe this to be true. The "first fine", etc.
"The hounds of swat are on the wobbles wip wop." Mag-
nificent sound. Now as a matter of fact I tried to read
A.C.S. to the small cousin and broke down lamentably.
The constant influx of "wrong words" put me out of it
altogether.

And Browning is full of jejune remarks about God.
And only parts of Landor are left us. And Elis says the
girl will be no use to me whatsoever. (Neither she may,
perhaps.) But who is any use to me? Hackett I see once
a month in a state of exhaustion, i.e. H. in a state of exhaustion. He makes two negative but intelligent remarks,
and departs before the conversation develops. Your
spouse is afar from us both. We are surrounded by live
stock.

I enjoy certain animal contacts.... without malice. I
have a "nice disposition". I pat them like so many re-
trievers.... *ebbene?* I live as a man among herds.... for
which I have a considerate, or at least considerable, if

misplaced, affection. "Herds" is possibly a misnomer. A litter of pups that amuses me. I am not prey to William's hostilities.... save that I dislike ill-natured animals.

As for poetry: how the devil *can* anyone like it.... given, I mean, the sort of thing usually purveyed under that label?

The girl asked me the only sane question I have ever had asked me about it.

"But is there no one like Bach! No one from whom one can get all of it?"

That staves in my stratified culture.

The Odyssey? But she does not—naturally, she does not read greek. She is "wholly uneducated". That is to say I find her reading Voltaire and Henry James with placidity.

And Dante? But she does not read italian. Nor latin. And besides, Dante! One needs a whole apparatus criticus to sift out his good from his bad; the appalling syntax from the magnificence of the passion. Miss Mitford said "Dante is gothic". Out of the mouths of prudes and imbeciles! Gothic, involved, and magnificent, and a master of nearly all forms of expression. And what, pray, is one to reply to a person who after having read *La Maison Tellier*, refuses to stand "The fifth chariot of the pole, already upturning, when I who had, etc., ... turning as Pyramus whom when the mulberry had been tasted.... not otherwise than as, etc." The quotation is inexact, but I can not be expected to carry English translations of Dante about with me in a suit case. Dante is a sealed book to our virgin, and likewise Catullus, and Villon is difficult French.... and Sappho.... perhaps a little Swinburnian? *Ille mi par esse....* is possibly better than the Aeolic original; harder in outline. (If this bores you, give it to Elis.) Chaucer writes in a forgotten language. One must read earlier authors first, if one is to run through him with ease or with pleasure. What the devil is left us? What argument for a person too sincere to give way to the current mania for assenting to culture? The fanaticism of certain people who believe they ought to "read poetry" and "be acquainted with" art. A person, I mean, who has taken naturally to good prose; who is so little concerned with appearing educated that she does not know whether Shelley is a dead poet or still living, ditto, Keats. It is quite oriental. Ramdath told me a tale from the Mahabharata, but it was only when I found it in the Mahabharata that I discovered it had not happened to Ramdath's grandpapa. If people would forget a bit more, we might have a real love of poetry..Imagine on what delightful terms the living would compete with their forebears if the doriphory of death were once, for even a week or so, removed from the "brows" or "works" of the "standard" authors. No more Job and Stock's "Works of the Poets", series including Mrs Hemans, Proctor and Cowper 7/6, 5/-, 2/6, hymn-book-padded-leather with gilding, real cloth *with* gilding, plain covers. The great Victorian age has done even better. Culture, utility!! I found in lodgings a tin biscuit-box, an adornment. It represented a bundle of books, of equal size, bound in leather, a series, the spiritual legacy of an era, education, popularity. The titles of the tin books were as follows:

History of England
Pilgrim's Progress
Burns
Pickwick Papers
Robinson Crusoe
Gulliver's Travels
Self-Help
Shakespeare.

Is it any wonder we have Gosse cautioning us against De Maupassant's account of Swinburne, and saying that De M's unbridled fancy gave great offence when it reached the recluse at Putney. Or dribbling, i.e. Gosse dribbling along about "events at the Art Club which were *widely discussed at the time*" (italics mine) when he might have said simply "Algernon got drunk and stove in all the hats in the cloak-room".

Yours,
Walter Villerant

3. WALTER VILLERANT TO MRS BLAND BURN

My dear Lydia,

Levine is a clever man. Yes "of course", of course I agree with you. He is a clever man. He is constantly being referred to, by Cincinnati papers, as the "brains behind the female suffrage movement in England" or the "brains behind" the neo-vegetarians or the "brains behind" the reformed simple-lifers. Were he in France he would undoubtedly get himself referred to as the brains behind the Claudel pseudo-romantico-tholocoes. All things are grist to his mill. He knows the psychological moment: i.e. when a given idea or "form" will fetch the maximum price per thousand. I don't wonder William wants you to get rid of him.

There is no reason why William should see him, there is no reason why William should not punch his face in an orgy of sensuous gratification, there is no reason why William should not kick him downstairs. There is no reason why any one should see him, or hear him, or endure him. And there is no reason why I should not see him. Besides he once procured me £12. I use the word "procure" with intention. It applies—temperamentally it applies to all of his acts: does he write, does he commission an article, it is all, in some way, procuration.

On the whole, I do not even dislike him. He has unbounded naïveté. I am a civilized man; I can put up with anything that amuses me.

As for the french pseudo-catholicians, ages of faith, Jeanne d'Arc canonized, capitalized and the rest of it. They are a pestilent evil. The procurer is an honest... and boastful... tradesman in comparison. And they are on the whole rotten writers.

"But pray what sort of a gentleman is the devil? For I have heard some of our officers say there is no such person; and that it is only a trick of the parsons, to prevent their being broke. For if it was publicly known that there was no devil the parsons would be no more use than we are in times of peace."

Said the serjeant. Fielding would not have put up with their dribble. And he was quite as good as the Russians. The Russians and half Flaubert thrown in. And he is as modern as the last vorticist writers:

"First having planted her right eye side-ways against Mr. Jones....."

Not having been at Rugby or Eton, I can take up anglophilia as a decent and defendable bastion, and leave William to enthuse over moujiks. I believe there is just as much good... no, dear lady, I forget myself or rather I forget I am not writing to William, and that this is not the siècle de Brantôme. I "believe" there is just as much animal energy latent.... or patent in the inhabitants of your esteemed chalk hummock. At any rate I was born in a more nervous and arid climate.

De Gourmont is dead, and with him has ceased Monsieur Croquant, and I suppose the washy rhetoricians, this back-flush of dead symbolism, dead celticism, etc., will have its or their way, their ways, south of the channel. There seems no one to stop it. The "sociétés" will be full of it. The french mystic is the most footling of all mystics. France herself will go under. I mean France as the arbitress of our literary destinies, the light we look to, from our penumbra. Or perhaps Dr Duhamel, with his realism of hospitals, and the brilliant, long silent Romains, the humane Vildrac will save us? Damn Romain Rolland. Charles-Louis Philippe is excessive. Meritorious, doubtless, but excessive.

Amitiés,

Walter

12 April 1917.

4. W. VILLERANT TO THE EX-MRS BURN

My dear Lydia,

Stupidity is a pest, a baccillus, an infection, a raging lion that does not stay in one place but perambulates. When two fools meet, a third springs up instanter between them, a composite worse than either begetter. We see the young of both sexes, and of your sex which is the more fluid, sunk into amalgams; into domestic and communal amalgams.

I call on the sisters Randall, they are in the studio next to their own, seeking companionship. I am deluged with an half hour's inanity, breezy, cheerful inanity, replies that were "bright" in '92, replies that are modelled upon the replies in short stories.

People imagine that to speak suddenly, and without thinking beforehand, is to be brilliant. It feels so. The elder Faxton writes stories that would have been daring, in the days of Ibsen's adolescence. The Sœurs Randall return to their studio, a brace of callers is waiting. I am deluged again with inanity, bright, cheery inanity. I flee waving metaphorical arms like a windmill.

Because of amalgams, Bohemias are worth avoiding. The poor ones are like pools full of frogs' eggs, and hordes of these globules perish annually. I mean they merge into suburbias.

Of the crop thrust yearly upon the metropolis some dry, others through small fault of intellect, through, perhaps, no defect of passion, but merely because of some natal commonness, some need to plunge back, to bathe in the second rate, subside into suburbias.

You say "What is suburbia?" You quibble and suggest that I am interested in "Society". My dear Lydia, I know an elderish man, and a man just ceasing to be young, and one woman, who have rejected "Society", and two who are untroubled by it one way or the other. But I do not set it against suburbias. All things pass under the nose of my microscope. I am one man without a class prejudice. It is perhaps my only distinction. But Mayfair, let me say, is not stupid. Mayfair is, by contrast, fantastic. Fantastic arts have always come out of Mayfairs.

An eminent dramatist, I can not say a distinguished, but at least an eminent and eminently successful dramatist, travels from London to Mudros to tell a naval Lieutenant that his disapproves of the cut of my collar.

It partakes of Haroun-al-Raschid, and of the 17th century spark who set out to play ball against the gates of Jerusalem. Or by contrast I call on Mrs Herringham-Sheffington at the instigation of Lady Houter, who is absent. I wander in bored despair. I discourse at last, and at length, on a piece of Capo-di-Monte, the only notable thing in a room full of expenses.

I explain the relation of Capo-di-Monte to democracy. That evening I hear I insulted a whole faction, I have been guilty of endless séditions, I have desired an ignominious peace. I am not to dine with Mrs Hinchfield on Thursday, although this had been arranged.

This does not interest you, for you are not interested in nuances, nor in the precise meaning of words; also you have never encountered a duchess. Neither are they my habit, any more than are the native English keepers of fruit stalls. But I do not dislike them. There is one formed wholly on "The First Violin", a second rate novel published twenty-eight years ago, when she was on the borders of thirty. She has the mind of an American female music student, in a Münchner, or Viennese boarding house.

The other, two years her junior, has the mentality of a graduate from, let us say, Ogontz or some other highly-priced American female seminary. For a quarter of a century she has preserved this crepe-paper flower in an almost undusty condition.

My present char-woman wears velvet shoes, she wears pseudo-diamond combs at her dish-washing. The velvet shoes are laced with velvet ribbons, and her get-up is rather untidy. A fact which you will read without interest. But your friend Molly from Southport has seen the Lady Godiva buying two and a half yards of green ribbon in Burbages: "And making such a display of herself. And such a crowd of shop-assistants, and her mother, etc. . . ." Molly attempts to mimic Lady G's intonation and fails more pronouncedly.

"Such a display of herself." I am still in the dark as to why the Lady Godiva should not buy two and a half yards of green ribbon, or why her mother should not accompany her, or whether, for her quasi regality, she should purchase ribbon only in bales; or whether she should spend three quarters of an hour dressing for Burbages in some style recommended by Molly. The Lady Godiva is not displeasing to look at, affaire d'oculiste, a mind innocent, oh, innocent as a Christmas Annual, and of about the same texture.

(The peerage [female] is divided into two sections: the American section, which reads current novels; the British section, which reads "The Queen". It contains however several gracious and most charming people,—and not a few curiosities.) But this bores you. You have chosen. You will henceforth consort with Mollies. For the rest of your natural life. And you will take part in the cheery, bright.... automatic conversation of feminine studios.

Old Hinchbon is right for all that. I remember old Hinchbon meeting with Leffington whom he had known in his youth. I had also known Leffington in my twenties, twenty years later, and for six months or a year I drank in his anecdotal conversation, and thought him the best of good talkers. Mappen lasted three days. But Mappen is a "penseur". He is enflamed with ideas. He will tell you that he resembles Spinoza. He will compare his mind to that of Parmenides. And one must admit that he thinks. He has enough ideas for three days. After that he is finished. Anecdotes last a man longer. But a tonality such as Perringham's is durable for a lifetime. (All this is over your head.) Perringham's tonality, or his sense of style, makes him permanent company.

Of Hinchbon or old Leffington: "No. No. Leffington! It is no use. His conversation shows the effects of association, of continuous association with inferior people."

That is my allegorical answer, and you need not expect me at Pinner. You had your chance. You could not endure the high altitude. I do not write this out of malevolence. I do not mind your having a new husband, or a dozen. But there is a certain propreté, a certain fastidiousness of the mind. The old Slautzer used to mutter in the face of the British scrubbed-clean nut-ocracy...

We accepted her because she had once lived with a certain Viennese artist. She even passed for, and may have been actually, one of his various wives. That was her passport. She must have had some intelligence or he would not have stood her a week. She mumbled, she was hard to understand, I, on the whole, have very little to tell of her, but I can still hear her saying, as she waved a guardsman away from her table: "No, no, vot I say to dese people. Vot, I will zleep vit you. Yes, I vil zleep vit you. It is nossing. But talk to you half an hour. Neffair!! Vun musst traw de line SOMMEFVERE!!"

This fastidiousness of the mind, my dear Lydia, is something which I would recommend to you.

The old Slautzer did not attain it on all planes... notably on the plane of her finger-nails. And she never opened a window, or permitted a window to be opened, and she wore a greasy (but rich, very rich) fur-coat, indoors, out-of-doors, all the time.

There were certain things in her favour. But for constant immersion in second-rate conversation there is no extenuation whatever.

It may be that you have reached your habitat, but into that habitat you need not expect me to follow you. I do not mind your having a new husband, or a dozen new husbands, but that you have an inferior mental object is a desolating and discouraging matter. Not even by an hair's breadth would I impinge upon your new domesticities.

Yours,

Walter Villerant

5. MR. VILLERANT'S MORNING OUTBURST

My dear Imogene,

You ask me to "save him from the mire that sickens him". Really! ! I am tired of these operatic contortions. Est-ce qu'on exige la chasteté d'un homme vers sa quarantaine! Why mire? Why "sickens him"? There are plenty of quite nice young ladies; a little too sentimental perhaps; too religious; too domestic. They read you letters from sister Alice in the convent at Wicklow; above their atrociously belaced beds you are stared at by the photo-enlargement of the darling child; you are let in for the emotions of maternity; you are introduced to styles of furnishing which you hoped you had escaped once and for all when you escaped from the life of cheap lodgings; or you land a grade or two higher and are let in for reminiscence of the appalling dullness of some blasted suburban watering place when they had to stay there with their late husband (old army). Or once in the rarest of whiles you find affection and a temperament.

But why this animal should scribble to you about mire, and deck himself in the blatancies of repentance.... ajh!!

If he would pick his company and then inebriate, instead of inebriating and then picking his company! In short if he weren't a dogdasted fool, and likely to be a bore in all companies; if he weren't too full of sloth mental and physical to aspire to amateurs; if he would study the rudiments of physiognomy and make some sort of selection, SELECTION, my dear Imogene, which is even easier, even more practicable in acquaintances of the moment than in relationships inherited from one's family.... etc.... and let us have done with him.

In matters of this sort, as in all other human relations, a man takes his own mire with him, or his own disinfectants, or even his own free-air and sea-scape if he have a fortunate disposition.

True they are sometimes fussy when they think they are being imperious; this is the first mark of vulgarity, but it is a characteristic of all stupid women, and often triumphs over breeding. It is perhaps as common amid palatial surroundings as it is among the ambiguous.

Sincerely yours,

W. V.

6

No, my dear Caroline,

Russians!! Am I never to hear the last of these Russians! I have shut up the esteemed and estimable William, and now you take up the pillows.

The Russian (large R., definite article, Artzibasheff, Bustikosseff, Slobingobski, Spititoutski and Co. Amalgamated, communatated, etc.). "The Russian" my dear Caroline, is nothing but the western European with his conning-tower, or his top-layer, or his upper-story, or his control-board removed. As neither the governed Frenchman, nor Englishman (undermined by sentimentality, but still sailing in ballast), nor the automatic American, barge about in this rudderless fashion, one makes comparisons with the Russian "élan", Russian "vigour" etc.

Civilized man, *any* civilized man who has a normal lining to his stomach, may become Russian for the price of a little mixed alcohol, or of, perhaps, a good deal of mixed alcohol, but it is a matter of shillings, not a matter of dynamic attainment.

Once, and perhaps only once, have I been drunk enough to feel like a Russian. Try it, my dearest young lady, try it. Try it and clear the mind, free your life from this obsession of Russians (if Lenin and Co. have not freed you).

What are we told about Russians: vast humanity, brotherly love, above all, vast tolerance. All for a job lot of bottles. Note the attention to detail in: in Russian fiction, in Dostoïevsky, and in the next drunk you see brushing a non-extant crumb from the imaginary crease in his waistcoat. Precisely! Vast attention to detail, always detail uncorrelated with anything else. The drunk sits in his little clearing, he is enclosed by a vast penumbra of shadows, a penumbra of things dimly seen, he has infinite concern with some object within optical focus. (Vide Dostoïevsky.)

He has moments of phenomenal energy. At times his stride increases, he turns a corner with marvellous exactness of angle, and hits the wall six steps later. He tries to lift the policeman. He is filled with the blessings and beamings of tolerance.

I, my dear Caroline, a person dour enough in this climate, have observed myself mellow and human, I have observed myself practising fellowship, mingling with the products of democracy. In my normal West-European condition I can not talk to the English "lower-classes". I can converse with French peasants and workmen, I can play *bocchi* in the back-yard of a trattoria, but with the English of "different station" I am at loss for a subject. But Russian I am filled with invention. I will, by gad, I will pass myself off for a Frenchman. I do it triumphantly, liquor perhaps shielding my accent, I translate into broken English. The Tommy next to me in the "Tube" is returning to Amiens in the morning, we are full of mutual recognitions, I am his noble, his affectionate ally. He kisses me on both cheeks at departing. I present him with my last shilling. I had three-ha'pence in the morning, but these details are lost in a mist of humanity.

I have fathomed the Russians.

Yours eternally,
Walter Villerant

7

Hepsibah!

I decline to write of religion. Christianity as we understand it, i.e., as it is presented to our gaze in the "occident", has reduced itself to one principle:

"Thou shalt attend to thy neighbour's business in preference to thine own."

It is upon this basis that the churches are organized, it is upon this basis that they flourish, (bar one old established conspirator's club which exploits a more complicated scenic arrangement). They equally blame them-

selves on the victimized Galilean. Against all of which I
have no defence save the eleventh chapter of the Lun-Yu,
the 25th section.

Tseu-lou, Thseng-sie, Yan-yeou, and Kong-si-hoa were
seated beside the Philosopher, who said: "I am older than
you are but pay no attention to that in our conversations."

He continued, "We sit apart and in solitude, we are unrecognized, but if someone should recognize you, what
would you do about it?"

Tseu-lou replied lightly but respectfully: "Let us imagine a kingdom of ten thousand war-chariots, stuffed
in between other kingdoms, let them be full of levies, let
the first kingdom suffer death and famine; should your
friend (little Tseu-lou) be set in power, he would put
things right in less than three years; the people would
put on their courage."

The philosopher smiled at these words. And said: "And
you Thseng-sie?"

Thseng replied respectfully: "Let us imagine a province of sixty or seventy *li*, or even of fifty to sixty *li*, put
me in charge of it and in less than three years the people will have enough, and I will put the instruction in
rites and in music in charge of an exceptional man."

"And you Yan?" said the Master.

"I am not sure I could do these things, I should much
rather study. I should be happy in wearing the cobalt
robe of an acolyte in the great ceremonies at the Temple
of Ancestors, or in the public processions."

"And you Si-hoa?" said the Philosopher.

The last pupil picked a few odd chords on his viol, but
the sounds continued echoing in the bowl of it. He put
it aside and rose, and then said respectfully: "My opinion is entirely different from any among my companions".
The Philosopher answered "Who forbids you to express
it? Here each one may say what he likes".

Si-hoa continued: "The spring being passed over and
my spring clothes put in my chest, and wearing my com-

ing of age cap with five or six men and a half dozen
young chaps, I should like to go to the old swimming
hole on the Y, near Kou village, and feel the wind in
that country where they offer rain-sacrifice in the summer; and sing a little, and make a few tunes, and then
go back to my homestead".

The philosopher sighed, and added, "I am rather of
Si-hoa's opinion".

Three disciples took leave but Thseng-sie (presumably the Rodyheaver, or potential Xtn convert of the
company) remained and asked after an interval: "What
should one think of the speeches of these three disciples?"

Kung-fu-tseu said: "Each one has expressed his own
temperament. That is the end of the matter".

Yours,
Walter Villerant

And damn the occident anyhow!

8

My dear Imogene,

You! complain to me about Joyce's language. I will not
bother to answer, I will point merely to a recent article
on Joyce in *The Future* (an English periodical, not to be
confused with *Die Zukunft*). The author says, and I
think with reason, that wherever Joyce has made use of
lice, or dung, or other disgusting unpleasantness he has
done so with the intention, and with, as a considerable
artist, the result of heightening some effect of beauty, or
twisting tighter some other intensity.

The metal finish alarms people. They will no more
endure Joyce's hardness than they will Pound's sterilized
surgery. The decayed-lily verbiage which the Wilde

school scattered over the decadence is much more to the popular taste. Vomit, carefully labelled "Beauty", is still in the literary market, and much sought after in the provinces. I am not throwing that into contrast with Joyce's novels.

I have a much finer question, and one which I probably waste in sending you. It is of the contrast between Gautier and Baudelaire, so we are well up beyond the Wilde level.

I take it that art rises in some measure in proportion to its inimitability, even its untranslatability. And I have never found Gautier in English; nor do I see any ready means of saying

> Le squelette était invisible
> Au temps heureux de l'Art païen;
> L'homme, sous la forme sensible, etc.

in English.

"The skeleton was invisible in the happy era of pagan art", is felicitous, it is better than "happy time" or "happy days"; "era" has come to me as I write this, after years of thought on the matter. But I am not ready to translate Gautier into English. On the other hand I am praised by a confrère, who is anything but an absolute fool, for "vigour" in:

> One night stretched out along a hebrew bitch—
> Like two corpses at the undertakers—
> This carcass, sold alike to jews and quakers,
> Reminded me of beauty noble and rich.
> Although she stank like bacon in the flitch,
> I thought of her as though the ancient makers
> Had shown her mistress of a thousand acres,
> Casqued and perfumed, so that my nerves 'gan
> twitch. . . .

etc. I finished the sonnet without much mental effort in fifteen minutes of a May morning, threw away the MSS., and this is all that comes back to me. It seems fairly Baudelairian but is nowhere inevitable, nor does it seem to me greatly worth recovering.

Baudelaire had, we presume, a "message". He had also a function in the French verse of his time. The poetic language had grown stiff, even Gautier is less miraculous if one consider the tradition of French eighteenth century writing, the neatness of Bernard, (whom Voltaire addresses as "Gentil... dont la muse féconde, doit faire encore délices"...). The tone of

> Si tu ne peux vivre
> Sans un Apollon,
> C'est Anacreon
> Ami, qu'il faut suivre.
> Apprends à monter
> Ta galante lyre:
> Si tu veux chanter,
> Que Bacchus t'inspire
> Le tendre délire
> Que, cher à Thémire,
> S'en fait écouter.

had probably constricted French poetry, and there was doubtless need of some new shaggy influx.

But the Baudelairian "vigour" seems to me now too facile a mechanism. Any decayed cabbage, cast upon any pale satin sofa will give one a sense of contrast. I am not saying that Baudelaire is nothing but cabbages cast upon satin sofas, but merely that in many poems one "unpleasant" element is no more inevitable than another, and that for a great many of his words and lines other words and lines might be substituted; and that he can be translated very roughly without losing any of his quality.

The stuff looks more vigorous than it is.... As indeed bad graphic art often looks more skilful than it is....
Passons....

Villerant

P.S.—Bad Baudelaire in English has come from trying to do him in a lilies and clematis vocabulary, fitter for Alfred de Musset.

PAVANNES

PAVANNES

JODINDRANATH MAWHWOR'S OCCUPATION

The soul of Jodindranath Mawhwor clove to the god of this universe and he meditated the law of the Shastras.

He was a man of moderate income inherited for the most part from his fathers, of whom there were several, slightly augmented by his own rather desultory operations of commerce. He had never made money by conquest and was inclined to regard this method of acquisition as antiquated; as belonging rather to the days of his favorite author than to our own.

He had followed the advice of the Sutras, had become the head of an house in the not unprosperous city of Migdalb, in a quarter where dwelt a reasonable proportion of fairly honest and honourable people not unaverse to gossip and visits. His house was situated by a watercourse, in lieu of new fangled plumbing, and in this his custom was at one with that of the earliest Celts. It was divided in various chambers for various occupations, surrounded by a commodious garden, and possessed of the two chief chambers, the "exterior" and the "interior" (*butt* and *ben*). The interior was the place for his women, the exterior enhanced with rich perfumes, contained a bed, soft, luscious, and agreeable to the action of vision, covered with a cloth of unrivalled whiteness. It was a little humped in the middle, and sur-

mounted with garlands and bundles of flowers, which
were sometimes renewed in the morning. Upon it were
also a coverlet brightly embroidered and two cylindrical
pillows, one at the head and the other placed at the foot.
There was also a sort of sofa or bed for repose, at the
head of which stood a case for unguents, and perfumes
to be used during the night, and a stand for flowers and
pots of cosmetic and other odoriferous substances, es-
sences for perfuming the breath, new cut slices of lemon
peel and such things as were fitting. On the floor near
the sofa rested a metal spittoon, and a toilet case, and
above it was a luth suspended from an elephant's tusk,
uncut but banded with silver. There was also a drawing
table, a bowl of perfume, a few books, and a garland of
amaranths. Further off was a sort of round chair or tab-
ouret, a chest containing a chess board, and a low table
for dicing. In the outer apartment were cages for Jodindranath's birds. He had a great many too many. There
were separate small rooms for spinning, and one for carv-
ing in wood and such like dilettantismes. In the garden
was a sort of merry-go-round of good rope, looking more
or less like a May-pole. There was likewise a common
see-saw or teeter, a green house, a sort of rock garden,
and two not too comfortable benches.

2

Jodindranath rose in the morning and brushed his
teeth, after having performed other unavoidable duties
as prescribed in the sutra, and he applied to his body
a not excessive, as he considered it, amount of unguents
and perfumes. He then blackened his eyebrows, drew
faint lines under his eyes, put a fair deal of rouge on
his lips, and regarded himself in a mirror. Then having
chewed a few betel leaves to perfume his breath, and
munched another bonne-bouche of perfume, he set about
his day's business. He was a creature of habit. That is to

say, he bathed, daily. And upon alternate days he
anointed his person with oil, and on the third day he
lamented that the mossy substance employed by the earliest orthodox hindoos was no longer obtainable. He had
never been brought to regard soap with complaisance.
His conscience was troubled, both as to the religious and
social bearing of this solidified grease. He suspected the
presence of beef-suet; it was at best a parvenu and Mo-
hametan substance. Every four days he shaved, that is
to say, he shaved his head and his visage, every five or
ten days he shaved all the rest of his body. He meticu-
lously removed the sweat from his arm-pits. He ate three
meals daily; in the morning, afternoon and at evening
as is prescribed in the Charayana.

Immediately after breakfast he spent some time in-
structing his parrots in language. He then proceeded to
cock-fights, quail-fights and ram-fights; from them to the
classical plays, though their representations have sadly
diminished. He slept some hours at mid-day. Then, as is
befitting to the head of an house, he had himself arrayed
in his ornaments and habiliment and passed the afternoon in talk with his friends and acquaintance. The
evening was given over to singing. Toward the end of
it Jodindranath, as the head of his house, retaining only
one friend in his company, sat waiting in the aforemen-
tioned perfumed and well arranged chamber. As the
lady with whom he was at that time connected did not
arrive on the instant, he considered sending a messenger
to reproach her. The atmosphere grew uneasy. His friend
Mohon fidgeted slightly.

Then the lady arrived. Mohon, his friend, rose graciously, bidding her welcome, spoke a few pleasant words
and retired. Jodindranath remained. And for that day,
the twenty fifth of August, 1916, this was his last occupation. In this respect the day resembled all others.

This sort of thing has gone on for thirty five hundred
years and there have been no disastrous consequences.

3

As to Jodindranath's thoughts and acts after Mohon had left him, I can speak with no definite certainty. I know that my friend was deeply religious; that he modeled his life on the Shastras and somewhat on the Sutra. To the Kama Sutra he had given minute attention. He was firmly convinced that one should not take one's pleasure with a woman who was a lunatic, or leprous, or too white, or too black, or who gave forth an unpleasant odor, or who lived an ascetic life, or whose husband was a man given to wrath and possessed of inordinate power. These points were to him a matter of grave religion.

He considered that his friends should be constant and that they should assist his designs.

He considered it fitting that a citizen should enter into relations with laundrymen, barbers, cowmen, florists, druggists, merchants of betel leaves, cab-drivers, and with the wives of all these.

He had carefully considered the sizes and shapes and ancient categories of women; to wit, those which should be classified as she-dog, she-horse, and she-elephant, according to their cubic volume. He agreed with the classic author who recommends men to choose women about their own size.

The doctrine that love results either from continuous habit, from imagination, from faith, or from the perception of exterior objects, or from a mixture of some or all of these causes, gave him no difficulty. He accepted the old authors freely.

We have left him with Lalunmokish seated upon the bed humped in the middle. I can but add that he had carefully considered the definitions laid down in the Sutra; kiss nominal, kiss palpitant, kiss contactic, the kiss of one lip and of two lips (preferring the latter), the kiss transferred, the kiss showing intention. Beyond this he had studied the various methods of scratching and tickling, and the nail pressures as follows: sonorous, half moon and circle, peacock-claw, and blue-lotus.

He considered that the Sutra was too vague when it described the Bengali women, saying that they have large nails, and that the southern women have small nails, which may serve in divers manners for giving pleasure but give less grace to the hand. Biting he did not much approve. Nor was he very greatly impressed with the literary tastes of the public women in Paraliputra. He read books, but not a great many. He preferred conversation which did not leave the main groove. He did not mind its being familiar.

(For myself I can only profess the deepest respect for the women of Paraliputra, who have ever been the friends of brahmins and of students and who have greatly supported the arts.)

4

Upon the day following, as Jodindranath was retiring for his mid-day repose, his son entered the perfumed apartment. Jodindra closed the book he had been reading. The boy was about twelve years of age. Jodindra began to instruct him, but without indicating what remarks were his own and what derived from ancient authority. He said:—

"Flower of my life, lotus bud of the parent stem, you must preserve our line and keep fat our ancestral spirits lest they be found withered like bats, as is said in the Mahabharata. And for this purpose you will doubtless marry a virgin of your own caste and acquire a legal posterity and a good reputation. Still, usage of women is not for one purpose only. For what purpose is the usage of women?"

"The use of women," answered the boy, "is for generation and pleasure."

"There is also a third use," said his father, "yet with certain women you must not mingle. Who are the prohibited women?"

The boy answered, "We should not practise dalliance with the women of higher caste, or with those whom another has had for his pleasure, even though they are of our own caste. But the practise of dalliance with women of lower caste, and with women expelled from their own caste, and with public women, and with women who have been twice married is neither commanded us nor forbidden."

"With such women," said Jodindranath, "dalliance has no object save pleasure. But there are seasons in life when one should think broadly. There are circumstances when you should not merely parrot a text or think only as you have been told by your tutor. As in dialliance itself there is no text to be followed verbatim, for a man should trust in part to the whim of the moment and not govern himself wholly by rules, so in making your career and position, you should think of more things than generation and pleasure.

"You need not say merely: 'The woman is willing' or 'She has been two times married, what harm can there be in this business?' These are mere thoughts of the senses, impractical fancies. But you have your life before you, and perchance a time will come when you may say, 'This woman has gained the heart of a very great husband, and rules him, and he is a friend of my enemy, if I can gain favor with her, she will persuade him to give up my enemy.' My son, you must manage your rudder. And again, if her husband have some evil design against you, she may divert him, or again you may say, 'If I gain her favor I may then make an end of her husband and we shall have all his great riches.' Or if you should fall into misfortune and say, 'A liaison with this woman is in no way beset with danger, she will bring me a very large treasure, of which I am greatly in need considering my pestilent poverty and my inability to make a good living.'

"Or again: 'This woman knows my weak points, and if I refuse her she will blab them abroad and tarnish my reputation. And she will set her husband against me.'

"Or again: 'This woman's husband has violated my women, I will give him his own with good interest.'

"Or again: 'With this woman's aid I may kill the enemy of the Rajah, whom I have been ordered to kill, and she hides him.'

"Or again: 'The woman I love is under this female's influence, I will use one as the road to the other.'

"Or: 'This woman will get me a rich wife whom I cannot get at without her.' No, my Blue Lotus, life is a serious matter. You will not always have me to guide you. You must think of practical matters. Under such circumstances you should ally yourself with such women."

Thus spoke Jodindra; but the counsel is very ancient and is mostly to be found in the Sutras. These books have been thought very holy. They contain chapters on pillules and philtres.

When Jodindranath had finished this speech he sank back upon one of the cylindrical cushions. In a few moments his head bowed in slumber. This was the day for oil. The next day he shaved his whole body. His life is not unduly ruffled.

Upon another day Jodindranath said to his son, "There are certain low women, people of ill repute, addicted to avarice. You should not converse with them at the street corners, lest your creditors see you."

His son's life was not unduly ruffled.

AN ANACHRONISM AT CHINON

BEHIND *them rose the hill with its grey octagonal castle, to the west a street with good houses, gardens occasionally enclosed and well to do, before them the slightly crooked lane, old worm-eaten fronts low and uneven, booths with their glass front-frames open, slid aside or hung back, the flaccid bottle-green of the panes reflecting odd lights from the provender and cheap crockery; a few peasant women with baskets of eggs and of fowls, while just before them an old peasant with one hen in his basket alternately stroked its head and then smacked it to make it go down under the strings.*

The couple leaned upon one of the tin tables in the moderately clear space by the inn, the elder grey, with thick hair, square of forehead, square bearded, yet with a face showing curiously long and oval in spite of this quadrature; in the eyes a sort of friendly, companionable melancholy, now intent, now with a certain blankness, like that of a child cruelly interrupted, or of an old man surprised and self-conscious in some act too young for his years, the head from the neck to the crown in contrast almost brutally with the girth and great belly: the head of Don Quixote, and the corpus of Sancho Panza, animality mounting into the lines of the throat and lending energy to the intellect.

His companion obviously an American student.

Student: I came here in hopes of this meeting yet, since you are here at all, you must have changed many opinions.

The Elder: Some. Which do you mean?

Student: Since you are here, personal and persisting?

Rabelais: All that I believed or believe you will find in *De Senectute:* ". . . that being so active, so swift in thought; that treasures up in memory such multitudes and varieties of things past, and comes likewise upon new things . . . can be of no mortal nature."

Student: And yet I do not quite understand. Your outline is not always distinct. Your voice however is deep, clear and not squeaky.

Rabelais: I was more interested in words than in my exterior aspect, I am therefore vocal rather than spatial.

Student: I came here in hopes of this meeting, yet I confess I can scarcely read you. I admire and close the book, as not infrequently happens with "classics."

Rabelais: I am the last person to censure you, and your admiration is perhaps due to a fault in your taste. I should have paid more heed to DeBellay, young Joachim.

Student: You do not find him a prig?

Rabelais: I find no man a prig who takes serious thought for the language.

Student: And your own? Even Voltaire called it an amassment of ordure.

Rabelais: And later changed his opinion.

Student: Others have blamed your age, saying you had to half-bury your wisdom in filth to make it acceptable.

Rabelais: And you would put this blame on my age? And take the full blame for your writing?

Student: My writing?

Rabelais: Yes, a quatrain, without which I should scarcely have come here.

Sweet C. . . . in h. . . spew up some. . . .
(pardon me for intruding my own name at this point, but even Dante has done the like, with a remark that he found it unfitting)—to proceed then:

                          . . . . . .some Rabelais
To . . . . . and . . . . . and to define today
In fitting fashion, and her monument
Heap up to her in fadeless ex . . . . .

Student: My license in those lines is exceptional.

Rabelais: And you have written on journalists, rather an imaginary plaint of the journalists:

Where s. . . . . , s. . . . . and p. . . . . on jews conspire,
And editorial maggots . . . . about,
We gather . . . . -smeared bread, or drive a snout
Still deeper in the swim-brown of the mire.

O . . . . O . . . . . O b. . . . . . b. . . . . . b. . . .
O c. . . . . O . . . . O . . . . . .'s attire
Smeared with . . . .

Really I can not continue, no printer would pass it.

Student: Quite out of my usual . . . . . .

Rabelais: There is still another on publishers, or rather on *la vie litteraire*, a sestina almost wholly in asterisks, and a short strophe on the American president.

Student: Can you blame . . .

Rabelais: I am scarcely . . . . . . eh. . . . .

Student: Beside, these are but a few scattered outbursts, you kept up your flow through whole volumes.

Rabelais: You have spent six years in your college and university, and a few more in struggles with editors; I had had thirty years in that sink of a cloister, is it likely that your disgusts would need such voluminous purging? Consider, when I was nine years of age they put me in that louse-breeding abomination. I was forty before I broke loose.

Student: Why at that particular moment?

Rabelais: They had taken away my books. Brother Amy got hold of a Virgil. We opened it, *sortes,* the first line:

> *Heu, fuge crudeles terras, fuge litus avarum.*

We read that line and departed. You may thank God your age is different. You may thank God your life has been different. Thirty years mewed up with monks! After that can you blame me my style? Have you any accurate gauge of stupidities?

Student: I have, as you admit, passed some years in my university. I have seen some opposition to learning.

Rabelais: No one in your day has sworn to annihilate the cult of Greek letters; they have not separated you from your books; they have not rung bells expressly to keep you from reading.

Student: Bells! later. There is a pasty-faced vicar in Kensington who had his dam'd bells rung over my head for four consecutive winters, L'Ile Sonnante transferred to the middle of London! They have tried to smother the good ones with bad ones. Books I mean, God knows the chime was a musicless abomination. They have smothered good books with bad ones.

Rabelais: This will never fool a true poet; for the rest, it does not matter whether they drone masses or lectures. They observe their fasts with the intellect. Have they actually sequestered your books?

Student: No. But I have a friend, of your order, a monk. They took away his book for two years. I admit they set him to hearing confessions; to going about in the world. It may have broadened his outlook, or benefited his eyesight. I do not think it wholly irrational, though it must have been extremely annoying.

Rabelais: Where was it?

Student: In Spain.

Rabelais: You are driven south of the Pyrenees to find your confuting example. Would you find the like in this country?

Student: I doubt it. The Orders are banished.

Rabelais: Or in your own?

Student: Never.

Rabelais: And you were enraged with your university?

Student: I thought some of the customs quite stupid.

Rabelais: Can you conceive a life so infernally and abysmally stupid that the air of an university was wine and excitement beside it?

Student: You speak of a time when scholarship was new, when humanism had not given way to philology. We have no one like Henry Stephen, no one comparable to Helia Andrea. The rôle of your monastery is now assumed by the "institutions of learning," the spirit of your class-room is found among a few scattered enthusiasts, men half ignorant in the present "scholarly" sense, but alive with the spirit of learning, avid of truth, avid of beauty, avid of strange and out of the way bits of knowledge. Do you like this scrap of Pratinas?

Rabelais (*reads*):

’Εμὸς ἐμὸς ὁ Βρομίος.
Εμὲ δεῖ κελαδεῖν,
Εμὶ δεῖ παταγεῖν,
’Αν ὄρεα εσσύμενον

Μετὰ Ναίδων
Οἶα τε κύκνον ἄγοντα
Ποικιλόπτερον μέλος
Τᾶν ἀοιδᾶν. . . .

Student: The movement is interesting. I am "educated," I am considerably more than a "graduate." I confess that I can not translate it.

Rabelais: What in God's name have they taught you?!!

Student: I hope they have taught me nothing. I managed to read many books despite their attempts at suppression, or rather perversion.

Rabelais: I think you speak in a passion; that you magnify petty annoyances. Since then, you have been in the world for some years, you have been able to move at your freedom.

Student: I speak in no passion when I say that the whole aim, or at least the drive, of modern philology is to make a man stupid; to turn his mind from the fire of genius and smother him with things unessential. Germany has so stultified her savants that they have had no present perception, the men who should have perceived were all imbedded in "scholarship." And as for freedom, no man is free who has not the modicum of an income. If I had but fifty francs weekly . . . . . .

Rabelais: Weekly? C. . . . . J. . . . !

Student: You forget that the value of money has very considerably altered.

Rabelais: Admitted.

Student: Well?

Rabelais: Well, who has constrained you? The press in your day is free.

Student: C. . . . . J. . . . . !

Rabelais: But the press in your day is free.

Student: There is not a book goes to the press in my country, or in England, but a society of . . . . in one, or in the other a pie-headed ignorant printer paws over it to decide how much is indecent.

Rabelais: But they print my works in translation.

Student: Your work is a classic. They also print Trimalcio's "Supper," and the tales of Suetonius, and red-headed virgins annotate the writings of Martial, but let a novelist mention a privvy, or a poet the rear side of a woman, and the whole town reeks with an uproar. In England a scientific work was recently censored. A great discovery was kept secret three years. For the rest, I do not speak of obscenity. Obscene books are sold in the rubber shops, they are doled out with quack medicines, societies for the Suppression of Vice go into all details, and thereby attain circulation. Masterpieces are decked out with lewd covers to entoil one part of the public, but let an unknown man write clear and clean realism; let a poet use the speech of his predecessors, either being as antiseptic as the instruments of a surgeon, and out of the most debased and ignorant classes they choose him his sieve and his censor.

Rabelais: But surely these things are avoidable?

Student: The popular novelist, the teaser and tickler, casts what they call a veil, or caul, over his language. He pimps with suggestion. The printer sees only one word at a time, and tons of such books are passed yearly, the members of the Royal Automobile Club and of the

Isthmian and Fly Fishers are not concerned with the question of morals.

Rabelais: You mistake me, I did not mean this sort of evasion, I did not mean that a man should ruin his writing or join the ranks of procurers.

Student: Well?

Rabelais: Other means. There is what is called private printing.

Student: I have had a printer refuse to print lines "in any form" private or public, perfectly innocent lines, lines refused thus in London, which appeared and caused no blush in Chicago; and vice-versa, lines refused in Chicago and printed by a fat-headed prude—Oh, most fat-headed—in London, a man who will have no ruffling of anyone's skirts, and who will not let you say that some children do not enjoy the proximity of their parents.

Rabelais: At least you are free from theology.

Student: If you pinch the old whore by the toes you will find a press clique against you; you will come up against "boycott"; people will rush into your publisher's office with threats. Have you ever heard of "the libraries"?

Rabelais: I have heard the name, but not associated with strange forms of blackmail.

Student: I admit they do not affect serious writers.

Rabelais: But you think your age as stupid as mine.

Student: Humanity is a herd, eaten by perpetual follies. A few in each age escape, the rest remain savages, "That deyed the Arbia crimson." Were the shores of Gallipoli paler, that showed red to the airmen flying thousands of feet above them?

Rabelais: Airmen. Intercommunication is civilization. Your life is full of convenience.

Student: And men as stupid as ever. We have no one like Henry Stephen. Have you ever read Galdos' "Dona Perfecta"? In every country you will find such nests of provincials. Change but a few names and customs. Each Klein-Stadt has its local gods and will kill those who offend them. In one place it is religion, in another some crank theory of hygiene or morals, or even of prudery which takes no moral concern.

Rabelais: Yet all peoples act the same way. The same so-called "vices" are everywhere present, unless your nation has invented some new ones.

Student: Greed and hypocrisy, there is little novelty to be got out of either. At present there is a new tone, a new *timbre* of lying, a sort of habit, almost a faculty for refraining from connecting words with a fact. An inconception of their interrelations.

Rabelais: Let us keep out of politics.

Student: Damn it, have you ever met presbyterians?

Rabelais: You forget that I lived in the time of John Calvin.

Student: Let us leave this and talk of your books.

Rabelais: My book has the fault of most books, there are too many words in it. I was tainted with monkish habits, with the marasmus of allegory, of putting one thing for another: the clumsiest method of satire. I doubt if any modern will read me.

Student: I knew a man read you for joy of the words, for the opulence of your vocabulary.

Rabelais: Which would do him no good unless he could keep all the words on his tongue. Tell me, can you read them, they are often merely piled up in heaps.

Student: I confess that I can not. I take a page and then stop.

Rabelais: Allegory, all damnable allegory! And can you read Brantôme?

Student: I can read a fair chunk of Brantôme. The repetition is wearing.

Rabelais: And you think your age is as stupid as mine? Even letters are better, a critical sense is developed.

Student: We lack the old vigour.

Rabelais: A phrase you have got from professors! Vigour was not lacking in Stendhal, I doubt if it is lacking in your day. And as for the world being as stupid, are your friends tied to the stake, as was Etienne Dolet, with an "Ave" wrung out of him to get him strangled instead of roasted. Do you have to stand making professions like Budé?!!

> Vivens vidensque gloria mea frui
> Volo: nihil juvat mortuum
> Quod vel diserte scripserit vel fecerit
> Animose.

Student: What is that?

Rabelais: Some verses of Dolet's. And are you starved like Desperiers, Bonaventura, and driven to suicide?

Student: The last auto-da-fe was in 1759. The inquisition re-established in 1824.

Rabelais: Spain again! I was speaking of . . .

Student: We are not yet out of the wood. There is no end to this warfare. You talk of freedom. Have you heard of the Hammersmith borough council, or the society to suppress all brothels in "Rangoon and other stations in Burmah"? If it is not creed it is morals. Your life and works would not be possible nowadays. To put it mildly, you would be docked your professorship.

Rabelais: I should find other forms of freedom. As for personal morals: There are certain so-called "sins" of which no man ever repented. There are certain contraventions of hygiene which always prove inconvenient. None but superstitious and ignorant people can ever confuse these two issues. And as hygiene is always changing; as it alters with our knowledge of physick, intelligent men will keep pace with it. There can be no permanent boundaries to morals.

Student: The droits du seigneur were doubtless, at one time, religious. When ecclesiastics enjoyed them, they did so, in order to take the vengeance of the spirit-world upon their own shoulders, thereby shielding and sparing the husband.

Rabelais: Indeed you are far past these things. Your age no longer accepts them.

Student: My age is beset with cranks of all forms and sizes. They will not allow a man wine. They will not allow him changes of women. This glass . . . . . .

Rabelais: There is still some in the last bottle. De-Thou has paid it a compliment:

> Aussi Bacchus . . . .
> Jusqu'en l'autre monde m'envoye
> De quoi dissiper mon chagrin,
> Car de ma Maison paternelle
> Il vient de faire un Cabaret
> Où le plaisir se renouvelle
> Entre le blanc et le clairet. . .
> On n'y porte plus sa pensée
> Qu'aux douceurs d'un Vin frais et net.
> Que si Pluton, que rièn ne tente,
> Vouloit se payer de raison,
> Et permettre à mon Ombre errante
> De faire un tour à ma Maison;
> Quelque prix que j'eu püsse attendre,
> Ce seroit mon premier souhait
> De la louer ou de la vendre,
> Pour l'usage que l'on en fait.

Student: There are states where a man's tobacco is not safe from invasion. Bishops, novelists, decrepit and aged generals, purveyors of tales of detectives . . . . . .

Rabelais: Have they ever interfered with your pleasures?

Student: Damn well let them try it!!!

Rabelais: I am afraid you would have been burned in my century.

RELIGIO

or, The Child's Guide to Knowledge

WHAT is a god?

A god is an eternal state of mind.

What is a faun?

A faun is an elemental creature.

What is a nymph?

A nymph is an elemental creature.

When is a god manifest?

When the states of mind take form.

When does a man become a god?

When he enters one of these states of mind.

What is the nature of the forms whereby a god is manifest?

They are variable but retain certain distinguishing characteristics.

Are all eternal states of mind gods?

We consider them so to be.

Are all durable states of mind gods?

They are not.

By what characteristic may we know the divine forms?

By beauty.

And if the presented forms are unbeautiful?

They are demons.

If they are grotesque?

They may be well-minded genii.

What are the kinds of knowledge?

There are immediate knowledge and hearsay.

Is hearsay of any value?

Of some.

What is the greatest hearsay?

The greatest hearsay is the tradition of the gods.

Of what use is this tradition?

It tells us to be ready to look.

In what manner do gods appear?

Formed and formlessly.

To what do they appear when formed?

To the sense of vision.

And when formless?

To the sense of knowledge.

May they when formed appear to anything save the sense of vision?

We may gain a sense of their presence as if they were standing behind us.

And in this case they may possess form?

We may feel that they do possess form.

Are there names for the gods?

The gods have many names. It is by names that they are handled in the tradition.

Is there harm in using these names?

There is no harm in thinking of the gods by their names.

How should one perceive a god, by his name?

It is better to perceive a god by form, or by the sense of knowledge, and, after perceiving him thus, to consider his name or to "think what god it may be."

Do we know the number of the gods?

It would be rash to say that we do. A man should be content with a reasonable number.

What are the gods of this rite?

Apollo, and in some sense Helios, Diana in some of her phases, also the Cytherean goddess.

To what other gods is it fitting, in harmony or in adjunction with these rites, to give incense?

To Koré and to Demeter, also to lares and to oreiads and to certain elemental creatures.

How is it fitting to please these lares and other creatures?

It is fitting to please and to nourish them with flowers.

Do they have need of such nutriment?

It would be foolish to believe that they have, never-

theless it bodes well for us that they should be pleased
to appear.

Are these things so in the East?

This rite is made for the West.

AUX ETUVES DE WIESBADEN

A. D. 1451

THEY *entered between two fir trees. A path of irregular
flat pentagonal stones led along between shrubbery. Halt-
ing by the central court in a sort of narrow gallery, the
large tank was below them, and in it some thirty or forty
blond nereides for the most part well-muscled, with
smooth flaxen hair and smooth faces—a generic resemblance. A slender brown wench sat at one end listlessly
dabbling her feet from the spring-board. Here the water
was deeper.*

*The rest of them, all being clothed in white linen shifts
held up by one strap over the shoulder and reaching half-
way to the knees,—the rest of them waded waist- and
breast-deep in the shallower end of the pool, their shifts
bellied up by the air, spread out like huge bobbing cauli-
flowers.*

*The whole tank was sunken beneath the level of the
gardens, and paved and panelled with marble, a rather
cheap marble. To the left of the little gallery, where the
strangers had halted, an ample dowager sat in a perfectly circular tub formed rather like the third of an
hogshead, behind her a small hemicycle of yew trees
kept off any chance draught from the North. She likewise wore a shift of white linen. On a plank before her,
reaching from the left to the right side of her tank-hogs-
head, were a salver with a large piece of raw smoked*

*ham, a few leeks, a tankard of darkish beer, a back-
scratcher, the ham-knife.*

*Before them, from some sheds, there arose a faint
steam, the sound of grunts and squeals and an aroma of
elderly bodies. From the opposite gallery a white-bearded
town-councillor began to throw grapes to the nereides.*

Le Sieur de Maunsier: They have closed these places
in Marseilles, causa flagitii, they were thought to be
bad for our morals.

Poggio: And are your morals improved?

Maunsier: Nein, bin nicht verbessert.

Poggio: And are the morals of Marseilles any better?

Maunsier: Not that I know of. Assignations are equally
frequent; the assignors less cleanly; their health, I presume, none the better. The Church has always been dead
set against washing. St. Clement of Alexandria forbade
all bathing by women. He made no exception. Baptism
and the last oiling were enough, to his thinking. St.
Augustine, more genial and human, took a bath to con-
sole himself for the death of his mother. I suspect that
it was a hot one. Being clean is a pagan virtue, and no
part of the light from Judaea.

Poggio: Say rather a Roman, the Greek philosophers
died, for the most part, of lice. Only the system of empire,
plus a dilettantism in luxuries, could have brought mankind to the wash-tub. The christians have made dirt a
matter of morals: a son of God can have no need to be
cleansed; a worm begotten in sin and foredoomed to
eternal damnation in a bottle of the seven great stenches,
would do ill to refine his nostrils and unfit himself for
his future. For the elect and the rejected alike, washing
is either noxious or useless—they must be transcendent
at all costs. The rest of the world must be like them;
they therefore look after our morals. Yet this last term
is wholly elastic. There is no system which has not been

tried, wedlock or unwedlock, a breeding on one mare or on many; all with equal success, with equal flaws, crimes, and discomforts.

Maunsier: I have heard there was no adultery found in Sparta.

Poggio: There was no adultery among the Lacedaemonians because they held all women in common. A rumour of Troy had reached the ears of Lycurgus: "So Lycurgus thought also there were many foolish vain joys and fancies, in the laws and orders of other nations, touching marriage: seeing they caused their bitches and mares to be lined and covered with the fairest dogs and goodliest stallions that might be gotten, praying and paying the maisters and owners of the same: and kept their wives notwithstanding shut up safe under lock and key, for fear lest other than themselves might get them with child, although themselves were sickly, feeble-brained, extreme old." I think I quote rightly from Plutarch. The girls of Lacedaemon played naked before the young men, that their defects should be remedied rather than hidden. A man first went by stealth to his mistress, and this for a long space of time; thus learning address and silence. For better breeding Lycurgus would not have children the property of any one man, but sought only that they should be born of the lustiest women, begotten of the most vigorous seed.

Maunsier: Christianity would put an end to all that, yet I think there was some trace left in the *lex Germanica,* and some in our Provençal love customs; for under the first a woman kept whatever man she liked, so long as she fancied: the children being brought up by her brothers, being a part of the female family, *cognati.* The chivalric system is smothered with mysticism, and is focussed all upon pleasure, but the habit of older folk-custom is at the base of its freedoms, its debates were on matters of modus.

These girls look very well in their shifts. They confound the precepts of temperance.

Poggio: I have walked and ridden through Europe, annoting, observing. I am interested in food and the animal.

There was, before I left Rome, a black woman for sale in the market. Her breasts stuck out like great funnels, her shoulders were rounded like basins, her biceps was that of a wheel-wright; these upper portions of her, to say nothing of her flattened-in face, were disgusting and hideous, but she had a belly like Venus, from below the breasts to the crotch she was like a splendid Greek fragment. She came of a tropical meat-eating tribe. I observe that graminivorous and fruit-eating races have shrunken arms and shoulders, narrow backs and weakly distended stomachs. Much beer enlarges the girth in old age, at a time when the form in any case, might have ceased to give pleasure. The men of this nubian tribe were not lovely; they were shaped rather like almonds: the curious roundness in the front aspect, a gradual sloping-in toward the feet, a very great muscular power, a silhouette not unlike that of an egg, or perhaps more like that of a tadpole.

Civilized man grows more frog-like, his members become departmental.

Maunsier: But fixed. Man falls into a set gamut of types. His thoughts also. The informed and the uninformed, the clodhopper and the civilian are equally incapable of trusting an unwonted appearance. Last week I met an exception, and for that cause the matter is now in my mind, and I am, as they say "forming conclusions." The exception, an Englishman, had found a parochial beauty in Savoia, in the inn of a mountain town, a "local character" as he called her. He could not describe her features with any minute precision, but she wore, he remembered, a dress tied up with innumerable small bits of ribbon in long narrow bow-knots, limp, hanging like grass-blades caught in the middle. She came into him as a sort of exhibit. He kissed her hand. She sat by his bedside and conversed with him pleasantly. They were quite alone for some time. Nothing more happened. From something in his manner, I am inclined to believe him. He was convinced that nothing more ever did happen.

Poggio: Men have a curious desire for uniformity. Bawdry and religion are all one before it.

Maunsier: They call it the road to salvation.

Poggio: They ruin the shape of life for a dogmatic exterior. What dignity have we over the beasts, save to be once, and to be irreplaceable!

I myself am a rag-bag, a mass of sights and citations, but I will not beat down life for the sake of a model.

Maunsier: Would you be "without an ideal?"

Poggio: Is beauty an ideal like the rest? I confess I see the need of no other. When I read that from the breast of the Princess Hellene there was cast a cup of "white gold," the sculptor finding no better model; and that this cup was long shown in the temple at Lyndos, which is in the island of Rhodes; or when I read, as I think is the textual order, first of the cup and then of its origin, there comes upon me a discontent with human imperfection. I am no longer left in the "slough of the senses," but am full of heroic life, for the instant. The sap mounts in the twigs of my being.

The visions of the mystics give them like courage, it may be.

Maunsier: My poor uncle, he will talk of the slough of the senses and the "loathsome pit of contentment." His "ideas" are with other men's conduct. He seeks to set bounds to their actions.

I cannot make out the mystics; nor how far we may trust to our senses, and how far to sudden sights that come from within us, or at least seem to spring up within us: a mirage, an elf-music; and how far we are prey to the written word.

Poggio: I have seen many women in dreams, surpassing most mortal women, but I doubt if I have on their account been stirred to more thoughts of beauty, than I have had meditating upon that passage in latin, concerning the temple of Pallas at Lyndos and its memorial cup of white gold. I do not count myself among Plato's disciples.

Maunsier: And yet it is forced upon us that all these things breed their fanatics; that even a style might become a religion and breed bigots as many, and pestilent.

Poggio: Our blessing is to live in an age when some can hold a fair balance. It can not last; many are half-drunk with freedom; a greed for taxes at Rome will raise up envy, a cultivated court will disappear in the ensuing reaction. We are fortunate to live in the wink, the eye of mankind is open; for an instant, hardly more than an instant. Men are prized for being unique. I do not mean merely fantastic. That is to say there are a few of us who can prize a man for thinking, in himself, rather than for a passion to make others think with him.

Perhaps you are right about style; an established style could be as much a nuisance as any other establishment. Yet there must be a reputable normal. Tacitus is too crabbed. The rhetoricians ruined the empire. Let us go on to our baths.

STARK REALISM—This Little Pig Went to Market

(*A Search for the National Type*)

THIS little American went to Vienna. He said it was "Gawd's Öwne City." He knew all the bath-houses and dance halls. He was there for a week. He never forgot it— No, not even when he became a Captain in the Great American Navy and spent six months in Samoa.

This little American went West—to the Middle-West, where he came from. He smoked cigars, for cigarettes are illegal in Indiana, that land where Lew Wallace died, that land of the literary tradition. He ate pie of all sorts, and read the daily papers—especially those of strong local interest. He despised European culture as an indiscriminate whole.

Peace to his ashes.

This little American went to the great city Manhattan. He made two dollars and a half per week. He saw the sheeny girls on the East Side who lunch on two cents worth of bread and sausages, and dress with a flash on the remainder. He nearly died of it. Then he got a rise. He made fifteen dollars per week selling insurance. He wore a monocle with a tortoise-shell rim. He dressed up to "Bond St." No lord in The Row has surpassed him.

He was a damn good fellow.

This little American went to Oxford. He rented Oscar's late rooms. He talked about the nature of the Beautiful. He swam in the wake of Santayana. He had a great cut glass bowl full of lilies. He believed in Sin. His life was immaculate. He was the last convert to catholicism.

This little American had always been adored—and quite silent. He was bashful. He rowed on his college crew. He had a bright pink complexion. He was a dealer in bonds, but not really wicked. He would walk into a man's office and say: "Do you want any stock? . . eh . . . . eh . . I don't know anything about it. They say it's all right." Some people like that sort of thing; though it is not the "ideal business man" as you read of him in *Success* and in Mr. Lorimer's papers.

This little American had rotten luck; he was educated—
soundly and thoroughly educated. His mother always
bought his underwear by the dozen, so that he should be
thoroughly supplied. He went from bad to worse, and
ended as a dishwasher; always sober and industrious; he
began as paymaster in a copper mine. He made hollow
tiles in Michigan.

His end was judicious.

This little American spoke through his nose, because he
had catarrh or consumption. His scholastic merits were
obvious. He studied Roumanian and Aramaic. He married a papal countess.

Peace to his ashes.

TWELVE DIALOGUES OF
FONTENELLE

TWELVE DIALOGUES OF FONTENELLE

1. ALEXANDER AND PHRINÉ

PHRINÉ. You could learn it from all the Thebans who lived in my time. They will tell you that I offered to restore at my own expense the walls of Thebes which you had ruined, provided that they inscribe them as follows: Alexander the Great had cast down these walls, the courtezan Phriné rebuilt them.

Alexander. Were you so afraid that future ages would forget what profession you followed?

Phriné. I excelled in it, and all extraordinary people, of whatever profession, have been mad about monuments and inscriptions.

Alexander. It is true that Rhodope preceded you. The usufruct of her beauty enabled her to build a famous pyramid still standing in Egypt, and I remember that when she was speaking of it the other day to the shades of certain French women who supposed themselves well worth loving, they began to weep, saying that in the country and ages wherein they had so recently lived, pretty women could not earn enough to build pyramids.

Phriné. Yet I had the advantage over Rhodope, for by restoring the Theban walls I brought myself into comparison with you who had been the greatest conqueror in the world; I made it apparent that my beauty was enough to repair the ravages caused by your valour.

Alexander. A new comparison. You were then so proud of your gallantries?

Phriné. And you? Were you so well content with having laid waste a good half of the universe? Had there been but a Phriné in each of the ruined cities, there would remain no trace of your ravages.

Alexander. If I should ever live again I would wish to be an illustrious conqueror.

Phriné. And I a lovable conqueress. Beauty has a natural right to command men, valour has nothing but a right acquired by force. A beautiful woman is of all countries, yet kings themselves and even conquerors are not. For better argument, your father Philip was valiant enough and you also; neither of you could rouse the slightest fear in Demosthenes, who during the whole course of his life did nothing but make violent speeches against you; yet when another Phriné (for the name is a lucky name) was about to lose a case of considerable importance, her lawyer, having used his eloquence all in vain, snatched aside the great veil which half covered her, and the judges who were ready to condemn her, put aside their intention at the sight of her beauties. The reputation of your arms, having a great space of years to accomplish the object, could not keep one orator quiet, yet a fair body corrupted the whole severe Areopagus on the instant.

Alexander. Though you have called another Phriné to your aid, I do not think you have weakened the case for Alexander. It would be a great pity if . . . .

Phriné. I know what you are going to say: Greece, Asia, Persia, the Indes, they are a very fine shopful. However, if I cut away from your glory all that does not belong to you; if I give your soldiers, your captains, and even chance what is due to them, do you think your loss would be slight? But a fair woman shares the honour of her conquests with no one, she owes nothing save to herself. Believe me, the rank of a pretty woman is no mean one.

Alexander. So you seem to have thought. But do you think the rôle is really all that you made it?

Phriné. No. I will be perfectly frank with you. I exaggerated the rôle of a pretty woman, you strained over hard against yours. We both made too many conquests. Had I had but two or three affairs of gallantry, it would have been all quite in order, there would have been nothing to complain of; but to have had enough such affairs to rebuild the Theban wall was excessive, wholly excessive. On the other hand, had you but conquered Greece, and the neighbouring islands, and perhaps even part of lesser Asia, and made a kingdom of them, nothing would have been more intelligent nor in reason; but always to rush about without knowing whither, to take cities without knowing why, to act always without any design, was a course that would not have pleased many right-minded people.

Alexander. Let right-minded people say what they like. If I had used my bravery and fortune as prudently as all that, I should scarcely ever be mentioned.

Phriné. Nor I either, had I used my beauty so prudently. But if one wishes merely to make a commotion, one may be better equipped than by possessing a character full of reason.

2. DIDO AND STRATONICE

Dido. Alas, my poor Stratonice, I am unhappy. You know what my life was. I maintained so precise a fidelity to my first husband, that I burned myself alive to escape accepting another. For all that I have not escaped evil rumour. It has pleased a poet, a certain Virgil, to transform so strict a prude as I was into a young flirt, charmed by a stranger's nice face the first day she sees him. My whole story turned upside down! The funeral pyre is left me, I admit, but my reason is no more the fear of being forced into a second marriage; I am supposed to be in despair lest the stranger abandon me.

Stratonice. And the consequences might be most dangerous. Very few women will care to immolate themselves for wifely fidelity, if a poet, after their deaths, is to be left free to say what he likes of them. But, perhaps, your Virgil was not so very far wrong; perhaps he has unravelled some intrigue of your life which you had hoped to keep hidden. Who knows? I should not care to take oath about your pyre.

Dido. If there was the slightest likelihood in Virgil's suggestion, I should not mind being suspected; but he makes my lover Æneas, a man dead three centuries before I came into the world.

Stratonice. There is something in what you say. And yet you and Æneas seem to have been expressly made for each other. You were both forced to leave your native countries; you sought your fortunes with strangers—he a widower, you a widow: all this is in harmony. It is true you were born three hundred years after his death; but Virgil saw so many good reasons for bringing you together that he has counted time for a trifle.

Dido. Is that sensible? Good heavens, are not three hundred years always three hundred, can two people meet and fall in love, despite such an obstacle?

Stratonice. Oh, Virgil was very clever in that. Assuredly he was a man of the world, he wished to show that we must not judge other people's love affairs by appearance, and that those which show least are often the truest.

Dido. I am not at all pleased that he should attack my reputation for the sake of this pretty fable.

Stratonice. But he has not turned you into ridicule, has he? He has not filled your mouth with silliness?

Dido. Not in the least. He has recited me his poem. The whole part that concerns me is divine, almost to the slander itself. In it I am beautiful, I say very fine things about my fictitious passion; and if Virgil had been obliged in the Æneid to show me as a respectable woman, the Æneid would be greatly impoverished.

Stratonice. Well, then, what do you complain of? They ascribe to you a romance which does not belong to you: what a misfortune! And in recompense they ascribe to you a beauty and wit which may not have been yours either.

Dido. A fine consolation!

Stratonice. I am not sufficiently your intimate to be sure how you will feel this, but most women, I think, would rather that people spoke ill of their character than of their wit or their beauty. Such was my temperament. A painter at the court of my husband, the Syrian king, was discontented with me, and to avenge himself he painted me in the arms of a soldier. He showed the picture and fled. My subjects, zealous for my glory, wished to burn the picture in public, but as I was painted admirably well and with a great deal of beauty—although the attitude was scarcely creditable to my virtue—I forbade them the burning; had the painter recalled, and pardoned him. If you will take my advice, you will do likewise with Virgil.

Dido. That would be all very well if a woman's first merit were to be beautiful or to be full of wit.

Stratonice. I cannot decide about this thing you call the first merit, but in ordinary life the first question about a woman one does not know is: Is she pretty? The second: Is she intelligent? People very rarely ask a third question.

3. ANACREON AND ARISTOTLE

Aristotle. I should never have thought that a maker of ditties would have dared compare himself to a philosopher, to one with so great a reputation as mine.

Anacreon. You did very well for the name of philosopher, yet I, with my "ditties," did not escape being called
the wise Anacreon; and I think the title "philosopher"
scarcely worth that of "the wise."

Aristotle. Those who gave you that title took no great
care what they said. What had you done, at any time, to
deserve it?

Anacreon. I had done nothing but drink, sing, and wax
amorous; and the wonder is that people called me "the
wise" at this price, while they have called you merely
"philosopher" and even this has cost you infinite trouble:
for how many nights have you passed picking over the
thorny questions of dialectic? How many plump books
have you written on obscure matters, which perhaps
even you yourself do not understand very well?

Aristotle. I confess that you have taken an easier road
to wisdom, and you must have been very clever to get
more glory with a lute and a bottle than the greatest of
men have achieved with vigils and labour.

Anacreon. You pretend to laugh at it, but I maintain
that it is more difficult to drink and to sing as I have,
than to philosophize as you have philosophized. To
sing and to drink, as I did, required that one should have
disentangled one's soul from violent passions; that we
should not aspire to things not dependent upon us, that
we be ready always to take time as we find it. In short,
to begin with, one must arrange a number of little affairs
in oneself; and although this needs small dialectic, it is,
for all that, not so very easy to manage. But one may at
smaller expense philosophize as you have philosophized.
One need not cure oneself of either ambition or avarice;
one has an agreeable welcome at the court of Alexander
the Great; one draws half a million crowns' worth of
presents, and they are not all used in physical experiments though such was the donor's intention, in a word,
this sort of philosophy drags in things rather opposed to
philosophy.

Aristotle. You have heard much scandal about me down here, but, after all, man is man solely on account of his reason, and nothing is finer than to teach men how they ought to use it in studying nature and in unveiling all these enigmas which she sets before us.

Anacreon. That is how men destroy custom in all things! Philosophy is, in itself, an admirable thing, and might be very useful to men, but because she would incommode them if they employed her in daily affairs, or if she dwelt near them and kept some rein on their passions, they have sent her to heaven to look after the planets and put a span on their movements; or if men walk out with her upon earth it is to have her scrutinize all that they see there; they always keep her busy as far as may be from themselves. However, as they wish to be philosophers cheaply they have stretched the sense of the term, and they give it now for the most part to such as seek natural causes.

Aristotle. What more fitting name could one give them.

Anacreon. A philosopher is concerned only with men and by no means with the rest of the universe. An astronomer considers the stars, a physicist nature, a philosopher considers himself. But who would choose this last rôle on so hard a condition? Alas, hardly any one. So we do not insist on philosophers being philosophers, we are content to find them physicists or astronomers. For myself, I was by no means inclined to speculation, but I am sure that there is less philosophy in a great many books which pretend to treat of it, than in some of these little songs which you so greatly despise, in this one, for example:

> Would gold prolong my life
> I'd have no other care
> Than gathering gold,
> And when death came
> I'd pay the same

To rid me of his presence,
But since harsh fate
Permits not this
And gold is no more needful,
Love and good cheer
Shall share my care—
Ah—ah—ah—ah—
Shall share
My care.

Aristotle. If you wish to limit philosophy to the
questions of ethics you will find things in my moral works
worth quite as much as your verses: the obscurity for
which I am blamed, and which, if present perhaps in
certain parts of my work, is not to be found in what I
have said on this subject, and every one has admitted
that there is nothing in them more clear or more beautiful that what I have said of the passions.

Anacreon. What an error! It is not a matter of defining the passions by rule, as I hear you have done, but of
keeping them under. Men give philosophy their troubles
to contemplate not to cure, and they have found a method
of morals which touches them almost as little as does
astronomy. Can one hold in one's laughter at the sight
of people who preach the contempt of riches, for money;
and of chicken-hearted wastrels brought even to fisticuffs
over a definition of the magnanimous?

4. HOMER AND ÆSOP

Homer. These fables which you have just told me cannot be too greatly admired. You must have needed great
art to disguise the most important moral instruction in
little stories like these, and to hide your thoughts in
metaphor so precise and familiar.

Æsop. It is very pleasant to be praised for such art by you who understood it so deeply.

Homer. Me? I never attempted it.

Æsop. What, did you not intend to conceal profound arcana in your great poems?

Homer. Unfortunately, it never occurred to me.

Æsop. But in my time all the connoisseurs said so; there was nothing in the *Iliad* or in the *Odyssey* to which they did not give the prettiest allegorical meanings. They claimed that all the secrets of theology and of physics, of ethics, and even of mathematics were wound into what you had written. Assuredly there was difficulty in getting them unwrapped: where one found a moral sense, another hit on a physical, but in the end they agreed that you had known everything and that you had said everything, if only one could well understand it.

Homer. Lying aside, I suspected that people would be found to understand subtleties where I had intended none. There is nothing like prophesying far distant matters and waiting the event, or like telling fables and awaiting the allegory.

Æsop. You must have been very daring to leave your readers to put the allegories into your poems! Where would you have been had they taken them in a flat literal sense?

Homer. If they had! It would have incommoded me a little.

Æsop. What! The gods mangling each other, thundering Zeus in an assembly of divinities threatens Hera, the august, with a pummelling; Mars, wounded by Diomed, howls, as you say, like nine or ten thousand men, and acts like none (for instead of tearing the Greeks asunder, he amuses himself complaining to Zeus of his wound), would all this have been good without allegory?

Homer. Why not? You think the human mind seeks only the truth: undeceive yourself. Human intelligence has great sympathy with the false. If you intend telling the truth, you do excellently well to veil it in fables, you render it far more bearable. If you wish to tell fables they will please well enough without containing any truth whatsoever. Truth must borrow the face of falsehood to win good reception in the mind, but the false goes in quite well with its own face, for it so enters its birthplace and its habitual dwelling, the truth comes there as a stranger. I will tell you much more: if I had killed myself imagining allegorical fables, it might well have happened that most folk would have found the fables too probable, and so dispensed with the allegory; as a matter of fact, and one which you ought to know, my gods, such as they are, without mysteries, have not been considered ridiculous.

Æsop. You shake me, I am terribly afraid that people will believe that beasts really talked as they do in my fables.

Homer. A not disagreeable fear!

Æsop. What! if people believe that the gods held such conversations as you have ascribed to them, why shouldn't they believe that animals talked as I make them?

Homer. That is different. Men would like to think the gods as foolish as themselves, but never the beasts as wise.

5. SOCRATES AND MONTAIGNE

Montaigne. Is it really you, divine Socrates? How glad I am of this meeting! I am quite newly come to this country, and I have been seeking you ever since my arrival. Finally, after having filled my book with your name and your praises, I can talk with you, and learn how you possessed that so *naïve* [1] virtue, whereof the *allures* [1]

[1] Termes de Montaigne.

were so natural, and which was without parallel in even your happy age.

Socrates. I am very glad to see a ghost who appears to have been a philosopher; but since you are newly descended, and seeing that it is a long time since I have met any one here (for they leave me pretty much alone, and there is no great crowding to investigate my conversation), let me ask you for news. How goes the world? Has it not altered?

Montaigne. Immensely. You would not know it.

Socrates. I am delighted. I always suspected that it would have to become better and wiser than I had found it in my time.

Montaigne. What do you mean? It is madder and more corrupt than ever before. That is the change I was wishing to speak of, and I expected you to tell me of an age as you had seen it, an age ruled by justice and probity.

Socrates. And I on the other hand was expecting to learn the marvels of the age wherein you have but ceased to exist. But, men at present, do you say, have not corrected their classic follies?

Montaigne. I think it is because you yourself are a classic that you speak so disrespectfully of antiquity; but you must know that our habits are lamentable, things deteriorate day in and day out.

Socrates. Is it possible? It seemed to me in my time that things were already in a very bad way. I thought they must ultimately work into a more reasonable course, and that mankind would profit by so many years of experiment.

Montaigne. Do men ever experiment? They are like birds, caught always in the very same snares wherein have been taken a hundred thousand more of their species. There is no one who does not enter life wholly new, the stupidities of the fathers are not the least use to their children.

Socrates. What! no experiments? I thought the world

might have an old age less foolish and unruled than its youth.

Montaigne. Men of all times are moved by the same inclinations, over which reason is powerless. Where there are men there are follies, the same ones.

Socrates. In that case why do you think that antiquity was better than to-day?

Montaigne. Ah, Socrates, I knew you had a peculiar manner of reasoning and of catching your collocutors in arguments whereof they had not foreseen the conclusions, and that you led them whither you would, and that you called yourself the midwife of their thoughts conducting accouchement. I confess that I am brought to bed of a proposition contrary to what I proposed, but still I will not give in. Certain it is that we no longer find the firm and vigorous souls of antiquity, of Aristides, of Phocion, of Pericles, or, indeed, of Socrates.

Socrates. Why not? Is nature exhausted that she should have no longer the power of producing great souls? And why should she be exhausted of nothing save reasonable men? Not one of her works has degenerated; why should there be nothing save mankind which degenerates?

Montaigne. It's flat fact: man degenerates. It seems that in old time nature showed us certain great patterns of men in order to persuade us that she could have made more had she wished, and that she had been negligent making the rest.

Socrates. Be on your guard in one thing. Antiquity is very peculiar, it is the sole thing of its species: distance enlarges it. Had you known Aristides, Phocion, Pericles and me, since you wish to add me to the number, you would have found men of your time to resemble us. We are predisposed to antiquity because we dislike our own age, thus antiquity profits. Man elevates the men of old time in order to abase his contemporaries. When we lived we overestimated our forebears, and now our posterity esteems us more than our due, and quite rightly. I think the world would be very tedious if one saw it with perfect precision, for it is always the same.

Montaigne. I should have thought that it was all in movement, that everything changed; that different ages had different characteristics, like men. Surely one sees learned ages, and ignorant, simple ages and ages greatly refined? One sees ages serious, and trifling ages, ages polite, ages boorish?

Socrates. True.

Montaigne. Why then are not some ages more virtuous, others more evil?

Socrates. That does not follow. Clothes change, but that does not mean a change in the shape of the body. Politeness or grossness, knowledge or ignorance, a higher or lower degree of simplicity, a spirit serious or of roguery, these are but the outside of a man, all this changes, but the heart does not change, and man is all in the heart. One is ignorant in one age, but a fashion of knowledge may come, one is anxious for one's own advantage but a fashion for being unselfish will not come to replace this. Out of the prodigious number of unreasonable men born in each era, nature makes two or three dozen with reason, she must scatter them wide over the earth, and you can well guess that there are never enough of them found in one spot to set up a fashion of virtue and rightness.

Montaigne. But is this scattering evenly done? Some ages might fare better than others.

Socrates. At most an imperceptible inequality. The general order of nature would seem to be rather constant.

6. CHARLES V AND ERASMUS

Erasmus. Be in no uncertainty, if there are ranks among the dead, I shall not cede you precedence.

Charles. A grammarian! A mere savant, or to push your claims to extremes, a man of wit, who would carry it off over a prince who has been master of the best half of Europe!

Erasmus. Add also America, and I am not the least more alarmed. Your greatness was a mere conglomeration of chances, as one, who should sort out all its parts, would make you see clearly. If your grandfather Ferdinand had been a man of his word, you would have had next to nothing in Italy; if other princes had had sense enough to believe in antipodes, Columbus would not have come to him, and America would not have been beneath your dominion; if, after the death of the last Duke of Burgundy, Louis XI had well considered his actions, the heiress of Burgundy would not have married Maximilian, or the Low Countries descended to you; if Henry of Castile, the brother of your grandmother Isabel, had not had a bad name among women, or if his wife had been of an unsuspectable virtue, Henry's daughter would have passed for his daughter and the kingdom of Castile have escaped you.

Charles. You alarm me. At this late hour I am to lose Castile, or the Low Lands, or America, or Italy, one or the other.

Erasmus. You need not laugh. There could not have been a little good sense in one place, or a little good faith in another without its costing you dearly. There was nothing—to your great-uncle's impotence; to the inconstancy of your great-aunt—that you could have done without. How delicate is that edifice whose foundation is such a collection of hazards.

Charles. There is no way of bearing so strict an examination as yours. I confess that you sweep away all my greatness and all my titles.

Erasmus. They were the adornments whereof you boasted, and I have swept them away without trouble. Do you remember having heard said that the Athenian

Cimon, having taken prisoner a great number of Persians, put up their clothing and their naked bodies for sale, and since the clothes were greatly magnificent there was great concourse to buy them, but no one would bid for the men? Faith, I think what befell the Persians would happen to a good number of others if one detached their personal merit from that which fortune has given them.

Charles. What is personal merit?

Erasmus. Need one ask that? Everything that is in us, our mind, for example, our knowledge.

Charles. And can one reasonably boast of these things?

Erasmus. Certainly. These are not gifts of chance like high birth and riches.

Charles. You surprise me. Does not knowledge come to the savant as wealth comes to most who have it? Is it not by way of inheritance? You receive from the ancients, as we receive from our fathers. If we have been left all we possess, you have been left all that you know, and on this account many scholars regard what they have from the ancients with such respect as certain men show their ancestral lands and houses, wherein they would hate to have anything changed.

Erasmus. The great are born heirs of their father's greatness, but the learned are not born inheritors of the ancient learning. Knowledge is not an entail received, it is an wholly new acquisition made by personal effort, or if it is an entail it is so difficult to receive as to be worthy of honour.

Charles. Very well. Set the trouble of acquiring mental possessions against that of preserving the goods of fortune, the two things are quite equal; for if difficulty is all that you prize, there is as much in worldly affairs as in the philosopher's study.

Erasmus. Then set knowledge aside and confine ourselves to the mind, that at least does not depend upon fortune.

Charles. Does not depend? The mind consists of a certain formation of cerebrum, is there less luck in being born with a respectable cerebrum than being born son to a king? You were a man of great genius; but ask all the philosophers why you weren't stupid and logheaded; it depended on next to nothing, on a mere disposition of fibres so fine that the most delicate operation of anatomy cannot find it. And after knowing all this, the fine wits still dare to tell us that they alone are free from the dominion of chance, and think themselves at liberty to despise the rest of mankind.

Erasmus. You argue that it is as creditable to be rich as to show fine intelligence.

Charles. To have fine intelligence is merely a luckier chance, but chance it all is at the bottom.

Erasmus. You mean that all is chance?

Charles. Yes, provided we give that name to an order we do not understand. I leave you to decide whether I have not plucked men cleaner than you have; you merely strip from them certain advantages of birth, I take even those of their understanding. If before being vain of a thing they should try to assure themselves that it really belonged to them, there would be little vanity left in the world.

7. AGNES SOREL—ROXELANE

Agnes. To tell you the truth, I don't understand your Turkish gallantry. The beauties of the seraglio have a lover who has only to say: I want it. They never enjoy the pleasures of resistance, and they cannot provide the pleasures of victory, all the delights of love are thus lost to sultans and sultanas.

Roxelane. How would you arrange it? The Turkish emperors being extremely jealous of their authority have set aside these refinements of dalliance. They are afraid that pretty women, not wholly dependent upon them, would usurp too great a sway over their minds, and meddle too greatly in public affairs.

Agnes. Very well! How do they know whether that would be a misfortune? Love has a number of uses, and I who speak to you, had I not been mistress to a French King, and if I had not had great power over him, I do not know where France would be at this hour. Have you heard tell how desperate were our affairs under Charles VII; to what state the kingdom was reduced, with the English masters of nearly the whole of it?

Roxelane. Yes, as the affair made a great stir, I know that a certain virgin saved France. And you were then this girl, La Pucelle? But how in that case were you at the same time the king's mistress?

Agnes. You are wrong. I have nothing in common with the virgin of whom you speak. The king by whom I was loved wished to abandon his kingdom to foreign usurpers, he went to hide in a mountainous region, where it would have been by no means too comfortable for me to have followed him. I contrived to upset this plan. I called an astrologer with whom I had a private agreement, and after he had pretended to scan my nativity, he told me one day in Charles's presence that if all the stars were not liars I should be a king's mistress, and loved with a long-lasting passion. I said at once: "You will not mind, Sire, if I leave for the English Court, for you do not wish to be king, and have not yet loved me long enough for my destiny to be fulfilled." The fear which he had of losing me made him resolve to be king, and he began from that time to strengthen his kingdom. You see what France owes to love, and how gallant she should be, if only from recognition.

Roxelane. It is true, but returning to La Pucelle. What was her part? Was history wrong in attributing to a young peasant girl what truly belongs to a court lady and a king's mistress?

Agnes. Were history wrong on this point, it were no great wonder. However, it is true that La Pucelle greatly stirred up the soldiers, but I before that had animated the king. She was a great aid to this monarch, whom she found armed against the English, but without me she would not have found him so armed. And you will no longer doubt my part in this great affair when you hear the witness which one of Charles VII's successors has borne to me in this quatrain:

> "Agnes Sorel, more honour have you won in the good cause, our France, her restoration, than e'er was got by prayer and close cloistration of pious eremite or devout nun." [1]

What do you say to it, Roxelane? Will you confess that if I had been a sultana like you, and had I not had the right to threaten Charles VII as I did, he would have lost his all?

Roxelane. I am surprised that you should be so vain of so slight an action. You had no difficulty in gaining great power over the mind of your lover, you who were free and mistress of yourself, but I, slave as I was, subjugated the sultan. You made Charles VII king, almost in spite of himself, but I made Soliman my husband despite his position.

Agnes. What! They say the sultans never marry.

Roxelane. I agree, and still I made up my mind to marry Soliman, although I could not lead him into marriage by the hope of anything he did not already possess. You shall hear a finer scheme than your own. I began to build temples, and to do many deeds of piety. Then I appeared very sorrowful. The sultan asked me the reason over and over again, and after the necessary pre-

[1] François Premier.

liminaries and crochets, I told him that I was melancholy because my good deeds, as I heard from our learned men, would bring me no reward, seeing that I was merely a slave, and worked only for Soliman, my master. Soliman thereupon freed me, in order that I might reap the reward of my virtuous actions, then when he wished to cohabit with me and to treat me like a bride of the harem, I appeared greatly surprised. I told him with great gravity that he had no rights over the body of a free woman. Soliman had a delicate conscience: he went to consult a doctor of laws with whom I had a certain agreement. His reply was that the sultan should abstain, as I was no longer his slave, and that unless he espoused me, he could not rightly take me for his. He fell deeper in love than ever. He had only one course to follow, but it was a very extraordinary course, and even dangerous, because of its novelty; however, he took it and married me.

Agnes. I confess that it is fine to subject those who stand so on their guard 'gainst our empery.

Roxelane. Men strive in vain, when we lay hold of them by their passions we lead them whither we will. If they would let me live again, and give me the most imperious man in the world, I would make of him whatever I chose, provided only that I had of wit much, of beauty sufficient, and of love only a little.

8. BRUTUS AND FAUSTINA

Brutus. What! Is it possible that you took pleasure in your thousand infidelities to the Emperor Marcus Aurelius, the most affable husband, and without doubt the best man in Roman dominions?

Faustina. And is it possible that you assassinated Julius Cæsar, that so mild and moderate emperor?

Brutus. I wished to terrify all usurpers by the example of Cæsar, whose very mildness and moderation were no guarantee of security.

Faustina. And if I should tell you that I wished to terrify likewise all husbands, so that no man should dare to be a husband after the example I made of Aurelius, whose indulgence was so ill requited?

Brutus. A fine scheme! We must, however, have husbands or who would govern the women? But Rome had no need to be governed by Cæsar.

Faustina. Who told you that? Rome had begun to have madcap crochets as humorous and fantastical as those which are laid to most women's credit, she could no longer dispense with a master, and yet she was ill-pleased to find one. Women are of the identical character, and we may equally agree that men are too jealous of their domination, they exercise it in marriage and that is a great beginning, but they wish to extend it to love. When they ask that a mistress be faithful, by faithful they mean submissive. The rule should be equally shared between lover and mistress, however it always shifts to one side or the other, almost always to that of the lover.

Brutus. You are in a strange revolt against men.

Faustina. I am a Roman, and I have a Roman feeling for liberty.

Brutus. The world is quite full of such Romans, but Romans of my type are, you will confess, much more rare.

Faustina. It is a very good thing that they are. I do not think that any honest man would behave as you did, or assassinate his benefactor.

Brutus. I think there are equally few honest women who would have copied your conduct, as for mine, you must admit it showed firmness. It needed a deal of courage not to be affected by Cæsar's feeling of friendship.

Faustina. Do you think it needed less vigour to hold out against the gentleness and patience of Marcus Aurelius? He looked on all my infidelities with indifference;

he would not do me honour by jealousy, he took away from me the joys of deceiving him. I was so greatly enraged at it, that I sometimes wished to turn pious. However, I did not sink to that weakness, and after my death even, did not Marcus Aurelius do me the despite of building me temples, of giving me priests, and of setting up in my honour what is called the Faustinian festival? Would it not drive one to fury? To have given me a gorgeous apotheosis!—to have exalted me as a goddess!

Brutus. I confess I no longer understand women. These are the oddest complaints in the world.

Faustina. Would you not rather have plotted against Sylla than Cæsar? Sylla would have stirred your indignation and hate by his excess of cruelty. I should greatly have preferred to hoodwink a jealous man, even Cæsar, for example, of whom we are speaking. He had insupportable vanity, he wished to have the empire of the world all to himself, and his wife all to himself, and because he saw Clodius sharing one and Pompey the other, he could bear neither Pompey nor Clodius. I should have been happy with Cæsar!

Brutus. One moment and you wish to do away with all husbands, in the next you sigh for the worst.

Faustina. I could wish there were none in order that women might ever be free, but if there are to be husbands, the most crabbed would please me most, for the sheer pleasure of gaining my liberty.

Brutus. I think for women of your temperament it is much better that there should be husbands. The more keen the desire for liberty, the more malignity there is in it.

9. HELEN AND FULVIA

Helen. I must hear your side of a story which Augustus told me a little while ago. Is it true, Fulvia, that you looked on him with some favour, but that, when he did not respond, you stirred up your husband, Mark Antony, to make war upon him?

Fulvia. Very true, my dear Helen, and now that we are all ghosts there can be no harm in confessing it. Mark Antony was daft over the comedienne Citherida, I would have been glad to avenge myself by a love affair with Augustus; but Augustus was fussy about his mistresses, he found me neither young enough nor sufficiently pretty, and though I showed him quite clearly that he was undertaking a civil war through default of a few attentions to me, it was impossible to make him agreeable. I will even recite to you, if you like, some verses which he made of the matter, although they are not the least complimentary:

Because Mark Antony is charmed with the Glaphira,
[It was by that name that he called Citherida.]
Fulvia wants to break me with her eyes,
Her Antony is faithless, what? Who cries:
Augustus pays Mark's debts, or he must fear her.
Must I, Augustus, come when Fulvia calls
Merely because she wants me?
At that rate, I'd have on my back
A thousand wives unsatisfied.
Love me, she says, or fight. The fates declare:
She is too ugly. Let the trumpets blare.

Helen. You and I, then, between us have caused the two greatest wars on record?

Fulvia. With this difference: you caused the Trojan War by your beauty, I that of Antony and Augustus by the defect of that quality.

Helen. But still you have an advantage, your war was much more enjoyable. My husband avenged himself for an insult done him by loving me, which is quite common, yours avenged himself because a certain man had not loved you, and this is not ordinary at all.

Fulvia. Yes, but Antony didn't know that he was making his war on my account, while Menelaus knew quite well that his was on your account. That is what no one can pardon him. For Menelaus with all the Greeks behind him besieged Troy for ten years to tear you from Paris' arms, yet if Paris had insisted on giving you up, would not Menelaus, instead of all this, have had to stand ten years siege in Sparta to keep from taking you back? Frankly I think your Trojans and Greeks deficient in humour, half of them silly to want you returned, the other half still more silly to keep you. Why should so many honest folk be immolated to the pleasures of one young man who was ignorant of what he was doing? I cannot help smiling at that passage in Homer where after nine years of war wherein one had just lost so many people, he assembles a council before Priam's palace. Antenor thinks they should surrender you, I should have thought there was scant cause for hesitation, save that one might have regretted not having thought of this expedient long before. However Paris bears witness that he mislikes the proposal, and Priam, who was, as Homer tells us, peer to the gods in wisdom, being embarrassed to see his Cabinet divided on such a delicate matter, not knowing which side to choose, orders every one to go home to supper.

Helen. The Trojan War has at least this in its favour, its ridiculous features are quite apparent, but the war between Augustus and Antony did not show its reality. When one saw so great a number of Imperial eagles surging about the land, no one thought of supposing that the cause of their mutual animosity was Augustus' refusal to you of his favours.

Fulvia. So it goes, we see men in great commotions, but the sources and springs are for the most part quite trivial and ridiculous. It is important for the glory of great events that their true causes be hidden.

10. SENECA AND SCARRON

Seneca. You fill full my cup of joy, telling me that the stoics endure to this day and that in these latter ages you professedly held their doctrine.

Scarron. I was, without vanity, more of a stoic than you were, or than was Chrysippus, or Zeno, your founder. You were all in a position to philosophize at your ease. You yourself had immense possessions. The rest were either men of property or endowed with excellent health, or at least they had all their limbs. They came and went in the ordinary manner of men. But I was the shuttle of ill-fortune; misshapen, in a form scarcely human, immobile, bound to one spot like a tree, I suffered continually, and I showed that these evils are limited by the body but can never reach the soul of a sage. Grief suffered always the shame of not being able to enter my house save by a restricted number of doors.

Seneca. I am delighted to hear you speak thus. By your words alone I recognize you for a great stoic. Were you not your age's admiration?

Scarron. I was. I was not content to suffer my pangs with patience, I insulted them by my mockery. Steadiness would have honoured another, but I attained gaiety.

Seneca. O stoic wisdom! You are, then, no chimera, as is the common opinion! You are, in truth, among men, and here is a wise man whom you have made no less happy than Zeus. Come, sir, I must lead you to Zeno and the rest of our stoics; I want them to see the fruit of their admirable lessons to mankind.

Scarron. You will greatly oblige me by introducing me to such illustrious shades.

Seneca. By what name must they know you?

Scarron. Scarron is the name.

Seneca. Scarron? The name is known to me. Have I not heard several moderns, who are here, speak of you?

Scarron. Possibly.

Seneca. Did you not write a great mass of humorous and ridiculous verses?

Scarron. Yes. I even invented a sort of poetry which they call the burlesque. It goes the limit in merriment.

Seneca. But you were not then a philosopher?

Scarron. Why not?

Seneca. It is not a stoic's business to write ludicrous books and to try to be mirth-provoking.

Scarron. Oh! I see that you do not understand the perfections of humour. All wisdom is in it. One can draw ridicule out of anything; I could even get it out of your books, if I wished to, and without any trouble at all: yet all things will not give birth to the serious, and I defy you to put my works to any purpose save that for which they were made. Would not this tend to show that mirth rules over all things, and that the world's affairs are not made for serious treatment? I have turned your Virgil's sacred *Æneid* into burlesque, and there is no better way to show that the magnificent and the ludicrous are near neighbours, with hardly a fence between them. All things are like these *tours de force* of perspective where a number of separate faces make, for example, an emperor if viewed from a particular angle; change the view-point and the figure formed is a scoundrel's.

Seneca. I am sorry that people did not understand that your frivolous verses were made to induce such profound reflections. Men would have respected you more than they did had they known you for so great a philosopher; but it was impossible to guess this from the plays you gave to the public.

Scarron. If I had written fat books to prove that poverty and sickness should have no effect on the gaiety of the sage, they would have been perhaps worthy of a stoic?

Seneca. Most assuredly.

Scarron. And I wrote heaven knows how many books which prove that in spite of poverty, in spite of infirmity, I was possessed of this gaiety; is not this better? Your treatises upon morals are but speculations on wisdom, my verses a continual practice.

Seneca. Your pretended wisdom was not a result of your reason, but merely of temperament.

Scarron. The best sort of wisdom in the world.

Seneca. They are droll wiseacres indeed who are temperamentally wise. Is it the least to their credit that they are not stark raving? The happiness of being virtuous may come sometimes from nature, but the merit of being wise can never come but from reason.

Scarron. People scarcely pay any attention to what you call a merit, for if we see that some man has a virtue, and we can make out that it is not his by nature, we rate it at next to nothing. It would seem, however, that being acquired by so much trouble, we should the more esteem it: no matter, it is a mere result of the reason and inspires no confidence.

Seneca. One should rely even less on the inequality of temperament in your wise men, who are wise only as their blood pleases. One must know how the interiors of their bodies are disposed ere one can gauge the reach of their virtue. Is it not incomparably finer to be led only by reason; to make oneself independent of nature, so that one need fear no surprises?

Scarron. That were better if it were possible; but, unfortunately, Nature keeps perpetual guard on her rights. Her rights are initial movements, and no one can wrest them from her. Men are often well under way ere reason is warned or awakened, and when she is ready to act she finds things in great disorder, and it is, even then, doubtful if she can do aught to help matters. No, I am by no means surprised to see so many folk resting but incomplete faith upon reason.

Seneca. Hers alone is the government of men and the ruling of all this universe.

Scarron. Yet she seldom manages to maintain her authority. I have heard that some hundred years after your death a platonic philosopher asked the reigning emperor for a little town in Calabria. It was wholly ruined. He wished to rebuild it and to police it according to the rules of Plato's *Republic,* and to rename it Platonopolis. But the emperor refused the philosopher, having so little trust in divine Plato's reason that he was unwilling to risk to it the rule of a dump-heap. You see thereby how Reason has ruined her credit. If she were in any way estimable, men would be the only creatures who could esteem her, and men do not esteem her at all.

11. STRATO, RAPHAEL OF URBINO

Strato. I did not expect that the advice I gave to my slave would have such happy effects, yet in the world above it saved me my life and my kingdom altogether, and here it has won me the admiration of all the sages.

Raphael. What advice did you give?

Strato. I was at Tyre. All the slaves revolted and butchered their masters, yet one of mine was humane enough to spare me, and to hide me from the fury of the rest. They agreed to choose for their king the man who, upon a set day, should see the sun rise before any one else. They gathered in the plain, the whole multitude gluing their eyes to the eastern heaven, where the sun is wont to arise; my slave alone, in accordance with my instructions, kept his eyes toward the west. You may well believe that the others thought him a fool. However, by turning his back on them he saw the first rays of the sun which caught on a lofty tower, while his fellows still sought the sun's body in the east. They admired the subtlety of his mind, but he confessed that it was my due and that I was still among the living. They elected me king as a man descended of gods.

Raphael. I see that your advice was quite useful yet do not find it a subject for wonder.

Strato. All our philosophers here will explain to you that I taught my slave that the wise should ever turn their backs on the mob, and that the general opinion is usually sound if you take it to mean its own opposite.

Raphael. These philosophers talk like philosophers. It is their business to scoff at common opinion and prejudice; yet there is nothing more convenient or useful than are these latter.

Strato. From the manner in which you speak, one sees that you had no difficulty in complying with them.

Raphael. I assure you that my defence of prejudice is disinterested, and that by taking prejudice's part I laid myself open to no small ridicule. They were searching the Roman ruins for statues and as I was a good sculptor and painter they chose me to judge which were antique. Michael Angelo, my competitor, made in secret a perfect statue of Bacchus. He broke off one of the fingers, then hid the statue in a place where he knew we would dig. I declared it antique when we found it. He said it was modern. I based my opinion chiefly on the beauty of the work which, according to our rules, was well worthy of Grecian carvers. Irritated at contradiction I carried the matter further, and said it had been done in the time of Polycletus or Phidias. Then Michael Angelo brought out the broken irrefutable finger. I was greatly mocked for my prejudice, but what would I have done without prejudice? I was judge, and as judge one must make decisions.

Strato. You would have decided according to reason.

Raphael. Does reason ever decide? I should never have known by any process of reason to what age the statue belonged, I should have seen only its excellent beauty, then prejudice came to my aid, saying that a beautiful statue was ancient, or should be. With such a decision I judged.

Strato. It may well be that reason has no incontestable formulæ for things of such slight importance; but upon all questions of human conduct she has decisions quite sure. Unfortunately men do not consult them.

Raphael. Let us then consult her on some point and see if she will decide it. Ask her if we should weep or laugh at the death of our friends and relations. On one side she will say, "they are lost to you, therefore weep." On the other, "they are delivered from the miseries of this life, you should therefore be joyful." In the face of such answers from reason, we act as local custom decrees. We weep at her bidding, and we weep so thoroughly that we cannot conceive laughter as possible; or we laugh so thoroughly that tears seem out of the question.

Strato. Reason is not always so undecided. She allows custom to decide such matters as are not worth her attention, but think how many very considerable things there are upon which she has clear-cut ideas, and from which she draws consequences equally clear.

Raphael. Unless I am much mistaken there are very few of these clear ideas.

Strato. No matter, they alone are worthy of absolute trust.

Raphael. That cannot be, for reason offers us a very small number of set maxims, and our mind is so made as to believe in many more. The overplus of one's inclination to believe in something or other all counts on the side of prejudice, and false opinions fill up the void.

Strato. But what need to cast oneself into error? Cannot one keep one's judgment suspended, in these unprovable matters? Reason stops when she knows not which way to turn.

Raphael. Very true, she has no other secret means of

keeping herself from mistakes, save that of standing stock-still; but such a condition does violence to man's mind, the human mind is in movement, and it must continue to move. It is not every man who can doubt; we have need of illumination to attain this faculty, we have need of strength to continue it. Moreover doubt is without action and among mankind we must act.

Strato. Thus one should preserve the prejudices of custom in order to act like the next man, but destroy the habits of thought in order to think like the sage.

Raphael. Better preserve them all. You seem to forget the old Samnite's answer when his compatriots sent to ask him what should be done with the Roman army which they had caught in the Caudine forks. The old man replied that they should put them all to the sword. The Samnites thought this too cruel; he then said they should let them go free and unscathed, and in the end they did neither, and reaped the evil result. It is the same with prejudices, we must either keep the whole lot or crush them out altogether, otherwise those you have eliminated will make you mistrust those which remain. The unhappiness of being deceived in many things will not be balanced by the pleasure of its being an unconscious deceit, and you will have neither the illumination of truth nor yet the comfort of error.

Strato. If there were no means of escaping your alternative, one should not long hesitate about taking a side. We should root out all prejudice.

Raphael. But reason would hunt out all our old notions and leave nothing else in their place. She would create a species of vacuum. And how could one bear this? No, no, considering how slight an amount of reason inheres in all men, we must leave them the prejudices to which they are so well acclimatized. These prejudices are reason's supplement. All that is lacking on one side can be got out of the other.

12. BOMBASTES PARACELSUS AND MOLIÈRE

Molière. I should be delighted with you, if only because of your name, Paracelsus. One would have thought you some Greek or Roman, and never have suspected that Paracelsus was an Helvetian philosopher.

Paracelsus. I have made my name as illustrious as it is lovely. My works are a great aid to those who would pierce nature's secrets and more especially to those who launch out into the knowledge of genii and elementals.

Molière. I can readily believe that such is the true realm of science. To know men, whom one sees every day, is nothing; but to know the invisible genii is quite another affair.

Paracelsus. Doubtless. I have given precise information as to their nature, employments, and inclinations, as to their different orders, and their potencies throughout the cosmos.

Molière. How happy you were to be possessed of this knowledge, for before this you must have known man so precisely, yet many men have not attained even this.

Paracelsus. Oh, there is no philosopher so inconsiderable as not to have done so.

Molière. I suppose so. And you yourself have no indecisions regarding the nature of the soul, or its functions, or the nature of its bonds with the body?

Paracelsus. Frankly, it's impossible that there should not always remain some uncertainties on these subjects, but we know as much of them as philosophy is able to learn.

Molière. And you yourself know no more?

Paracelsus. No. Isn't that quite enough?

Molière. Enough? It is nothing at all. You mean that you have leapt over men whom you do not understand, in order to come upon genii?

Paracelsus. Genii are much more stimulatory to our natural curiosity.

Molière. Yes, but it is unpardonable to speculate about them before one has completed one's knowledge of men. One would think the human mind wholly exhausted, when one sees men taking as objects of knowledge things which have perhaps no reality, and when one sees how gaily they do this. However, it is certain that there are enough very real objects to keep one wholly employed.

Paracelsus. The human mind naturally neglects the sciences which are too simple, and runs after those more mysterious. It is only upon these last that it can expend all its activity.

Molière. So much the worse for the mind; what you say is not at all to its credit. The truth presents itself, but being too simple it passes unrecognized, and ridiculous mysteries are received only because of their mystery. I believe that if most men saw the universe as it is, seeing there neither *"virtues"* nor "numbers," nor "properties" of the planets, nor fatalities tied to certain times and revolutions, they could not help saying of its admirable arrangement: "What, is that all there is to it?"

Paracelsus. You call these mysteries ridiculous, because you have not been able to reach into them, they are truly reserved for the great.

Molière. I esteem those who do not understand these mysteries quite as much as those who do understand them; unfortunately nature has not made every one incapable of such understanding.

Paracelsus. But you who seem so didactic, what profession did you follow on earth?

Molière. A profession quite different from yours. You studied the powers of genii, I studied the follies of men.

Paracelsus. A fine subject. Do we not know well enough that men are subject to plenty of follies?

Molière. We know it in the gross, and confusedly; but

we must come to details, and then we can understand the scope and extent of this science.

Paracelsus. Well, what use did you make of it?

Molière. I gathered in a particular place the greatest possible number of people and then showed them that they were all fools.

Paracelsus. It must have needed a terrible speech to get that plain fact into their heads.

Molière. Nothing is easier. One proves them their silliness without using much eloquence, or much premeditated reasoning. Their acts are so ludicrous that if you but show like acts before them, you overwhelm them with their own laughter.

Paracelsus. I understand you, you were a comedian. For myself I cannot conceive how one can get any pleasure from comedy; one goes to laugh at a representation of customs, why should one not laugh at the customs themselves?

Molière. In order to laugh at the world's affairs one must in some fashion stand apart, or outside them. Comedy takes you outside them, she shows them to you as a pageant in which you yourself have no part.

Paracelsus. But does not a man go straight back to that which he has so recently mocked, and take his wonted place in it?

Molière. No doubt. The other day, to amuse myself, I made a fable on this same subject. A young gosling flew with the usual clumsiness of his species, and during his momentary flight, which scarcely lifted him from the earth, he insulted the rest of the barnyard: "Unfortunate animals, I see you beneath me, you cannot thus cleave the æther." It was a very short mockery, the gosling fell with the words.

Paracelsus. What use then are the reflections of comedy, since they are like the flight of your gosling, and since one falls back at once into the communal silliness?

Molière. It is much to have laughed at onself; nature has given us that marvellous faculty lest we make dupes of ourselves. How often, when half of our being is doing something with enthusiasm, does the other half stand aside laughing? And if need were we might find a third part to make mock of both of the others. You might say that man was made of inlays.

Paracelsus. I cannot see that there is much in all this to occupy one's attention. A few banal reflections, a few jests of scanty foundation deserve but little esteem, but what efforts of meditation may we not need to treat of more lofty matters?

Molière. You are coming back to your genii, I recognize only fools. However, although I have never worked upon subjects save those which lie before all men's eyes, I can predict that my comedies will outlast your exalted productions. Everything is subject to the changes of fashion, the labours of the mind are not exempt from this destiny of doublets and breeches. I have seen, lord knows how many, books and fashions of writing interred with their authors, very much in the manner that certain races bury a man with his most valued belongings. I know perfectly well that there may be revolutions in the kingdom of letters, and, with all that, I guarantee that my writings will endure. And I know why, for he who would paint for immortality must paint fools.

FONTENELLE'S TRANSLATION FROM HADRIEN

Ma petite âme, ma mignonne,
Tu t'en vas donc, ma fille, et Dieu sçache où tu vas;
Tu pars seulette, nuê, et tremblotante, Helas!
Que deviendra ton humeur folichone?
Que deviendront tant de jolis ébats?

CHRONICLES FROM *BLAST*

CHRONICLES FROM *BLAST*

1. "LEST THE FUTURE AGE . . ."

Lest the future age looking back upon our era should
be misled, or should conceive of it as a time wholly cultivated and delightful, we think it well to record occasional incidents illustrative of contemporary custom, following, in so far as is convenient, the manner of John
Boccacio. Let it then stand written that in the year of
grace, 1914, there was in the parish of Kensington a
priest or vicar, portly, perhaps over fed, indifferent to
the comfort of others, and well paid for official advertise-
ment and maintenance of the cult of the Gallilean . . .
that is to say of the contemporary form of that cult.

And whereas the Gallilean was, according to record, a
pleasant, well-spoken, intelligent vagabond, this person,
as is common with most of this sect was in most sorts the
reverse . . their hymns and music being in the last
stages of decadence.

The said vicar either caused to be rung or at least permitted the ringing of great bells, untuneful, ill-managed,
to the great disturbance of those living near to the
church. He himself lived on the summit of the hill at
some distance and was little disturbed by the clatter.

The poor who lived in the stone court-yard beneath the
belfry suffered great annoyance, especially when their
women lay sick. Protest was, however, of no avail. The

ecclesiastic had the right to incommode them. The entire neighbourhood reeked with the intolerable jangle. The mediaeval annoyance of stench might well be compared to it. We record this detail of contemporary life, because obscure things of this sort are wont carelessly to be passed over by our writers of fiction, and because we endeavour in all ways to leave a true account of our time.

We point out that these bells serve no purpose, no one pretends that they advance the cult of the Gallilean, no one pretends that a musical chime of bells would be less efficient. They serve as an example of atavism. Once such bells were of use for alarm, or told the hour to a scattered peasantry, or announced a service to a village without other chronometers, now they persist in thickly populated portions of our city, without use, without other effect than that of showing the ecclesiastical pleasure in aimless annoyance of others.

The three circumjacent temples of Bacchus debased, and the one shrine of Aphrodite popularis, lying within the radius of this belfry cause less discord and less bad temper among the district's inhabitants.

The intellectual status of this Gallilean cult in our time may be well judged when we consider that you would scarcely find any member of the clergy who would not heartily approve of this biweekly annoyance of the citizens. For in this place at least the ringers must enforce their consummate incompetence by pretending to practice their discords, which are, very likely, worse than any untrained hand could accomplish.

2. ON THE RAGE OR PEEVISHNESS WHICH GREETED THE FIRST NUMBER OF BLAST

The first number of BLAST which came to many as cooling water, as a pleasant light, was greeted with such a mincing jibber by the banderlog that one is fain to examine the phenomenon. The jibber was for the most part inarticulate, but certain phrases are translatable into English. We note thereby certain symptoms of minds bordering on the human. First that the sterile, having with pain acquired one ready made set of ideas from deceased creators of ideas, are above all else enraged at being told that the creation of ideas did not stop at the date of their birth; that they were, by their advent into this life, unable to produce a state of static awe and stolidity. The common or homo canis snarls violently at the thought of there being ideas which he doesn't know. He dies a death of lingering horror at the thought that even after he has learned even the newest set of made ideas, there will still be more ideas, that the horrid things will grow, will go on growing in spite of him.

BLAST does not attempt to reconcile the homo canis with himself. Of course the homo canis will follow us. It is the nature of the homo canis to follow. They growl but they follow. They have even followed things in black surtouts with their collars buttoned behind.

OYEZ. OYEZ. OYEZ.

Throughout the length and breadth of England and through three continents BLAST has been REVILED by all save the intelligent.

WHY?

Because BLAST alone has dared to show modernity its face in an honest glass.

While all other periodicals were whispering PEACE in one tone or another; while they were all saying "hush" (for one "interest" or another), "BLAST" alone dared to present the actual discords of modern "civilization," DISCORDS now only too apparent in the open conflict between teutonic atavism and unsatisfactory Democracy.

It has been averred by the homo canis that Blast is run to make money and to attract attention. Does one print a paper half a yard square, in steam-calliope pink in order to make it coy and invisible? Will Blast help to dispel the opinion of the homo canis, of the luminaries of the British bar (wet or dry), of the L.C.C. etc., that one makes one's art to please them?

Will the homo canis as a communal unit, gathered together in his aggregate, endure being deprived of his accustomed flattery, by Blast?

Does anything but the need of food drive the artist into contact with the homo canis?

Would he not retire to his estates if he had 'em? Would he not do his work quietly and leave the human brotherhood to bemuck the exchanges, and to profit by his productions, after death had removed him from this scene of slimy indignity?

The melancholy young man, the aesthetic young man, the romantic young man, past types; fabians, past; simple lifers past. The present: a generation which ceases to flatter.

Thank god for our atrabilious companions.

And the homo canis?

Will go out munching our ideas. Whining.

Vaguely one sees that the homo canis is divisible into types. There is the snarling type and the smirking. There was the one who "was unable to laugh" at the first number of Blast. The entrails of some people are not strong enough to permit them the passion of hatred.

3. LAWRENCE BINYON

We regret that we cannot entitle this article "Homage to Mr. Lawrence Binyon," for Mr. Binyon has not sufficiently rebelled. Manifestly he is not one of the ignorant. He is far from being one of the outer world, but in reading his work we constantly feel the influence upon him of his reading of the worst English poets. We find him in a disgusting attitude of respect toward predecessors whose intellect is vastly inferior to his own. This is loathesome. Mr. Binyon has thought; he has plunged into the knowledge of the East and extended the borders of occidental knowledge, and yet his mind constantly harks back to some folly of nineteenth century Europe. We can see him as it were constantly restraining his inventiveness, constantly trying to conform to an orthodox view against which his thought and emotions rebel, constantly trying to justify Chinese intelligence by dragging it a little nearer to some Western precedent. Ah well! Mr. Binyon has, indubitably, his moments. Very few men do have any moments whatever, and for the benefit of such readers as have not sufficiently respected Mr. Binyon for his, it would be well to set forth a few of them. They are found in his "Flight of the Dragon," a book otherwise unpleasantly marred by his recurrent respect for inferior, very inferior people.

P. 17. Every statue, every picture, is a series of ordered relations, controlled, as the body is controlled in the dance, by the will to express a single idea.

P. 18. In a bad painting the units of form, mass, colour, are robbed of their potential energy, isolated, because brought into no organic relation.

P. 19. Art is not an adjunct to existence, a reproduction of the actual.

P. 21. FOR INDEED IT IS NOT ESSENTIAL THAT THE SUBJECT-MATTER SHOULD REPRESENT OR BE LIKE ANYTHING IN NATURE; ONLY IT MUST BE ALIVE WITH A RHYTHMIC VITALITY OF ITS OWN.

On P. Fourteen he quotes with approbation a Chinese author as follows:—As a man's language is an unerring index to his nature, so the actual strokes of his brush in writing or painting betray him and announce either the freedom and nobility of his soul or its meanness and limitation.

P. 21. You may say that the waves of Korin's famous screen are not like real waves: but they move, they have force and volume.

P. 90. It would be vain to deny that certain kinds and tones of colour have real correspondence with emotional states of mind.

P. 91. Chemists had not multiplied colours for the painter, but he knew how to prepare those he had.

P. 94. Our thoughts about decoration are too much dominated, I think, by the conception of pattern as a sort of mosaic, each element in the pattern being repeated, a form without life of its own, something inert and bounded by itself. We get a mechanical succession which aims at rhythm, but does not attain rhythmic vitality.

E.P.

MADOX FORD AT RAPALLO

MADOX FORD AT RAPALLO

A CONVERSATION BETWEEN FORD MADOX FORD
AND EZRA POUND
(Translated by Olga Rudge)

FORD Madox Ford, "grandfather of contemporary English literature", founder of the *English Review*, the *Transatlantic Review*, friend of Henry James and Hudson, a collaborator of Conrad's, etc., passed through Rapallo the beginning of August, 1932. We were present when his friend Pound attacked him, verbally:

Pound: What authors should a young Italian writer read if he wants to learn how to write novels?

Ford: (Spitting vigorously) Better to think about finding himself a subject.

Pound: (Suavely, ignoring Ford's irritation) Well, suppose he has already had the intelligence to read Stendhal and Flaubert?

Ford: A different curriculum is needed for each talent. One can learn from Flaubert and from Miss Braddon. In a certain way one can learn as much from a rotten writer as from a great one.

Pound: Which of your books would you like to see translated into Italian and in what order?

Ford: I don't trust translations; they would leave nothing of my best qualities. Some writers are translatable.

Pound: What are the most important qualities in a prose writer?

Ford: What does "prose writer" mean? The Napoleonic Code or the Canticle of Canticles?

Pound: Let us say a novelist.

Ford: (In agony) Oh Hell! Say philosophical grounding, a knowledge of words' roots, of the meaning of words.

Pound: What should a young prose writer do first?

Ford: (More and more annoyed at the inquisition) Brush his teeth.

Pound: (Ironically calm, with serene magniloquence) In the vast critical output of the illustrious critic now being interviewed (changing tone) . . . You have praised writer after writer with no apparent distinction (stressing the word "apparent" nearly with rage). Is there any?

Ford: There are authentic writers and imitation writers; there is no difference among the authentic ones. There is no difference between Picasso and El Greco.

Pound: Don't get away from me into painting. Stick to literary examples.

Ford: Hudson, and Flaubert in "Trois Contes". Not all of Flaubert, let us say the "Trois Contes."

Pound: You have often spoken to me of "fine talents." Are some finer than others?

(Ford tries to evade a comparison)

Pound: Are there new writers on a level with Henry James and Hudson?

Ford: (After qualifying Henry James' talent at some length) Yes. Hemingway, Elizabeth Roberts, Caroline Gordon, George Davis. Read "The Opening of a Door" and "Penhelly".

Pound: But as artists? If James is a consummate artist, is Hudson something else? He may be called a pure prose writer, not a novelist.

Ford: The difference between weaving and drawing.

Pound: Now for the term "promising." What makes you think a new writer "promises"?

Ford: The first sentence I read. When two words are put together they produce an overtone. The overtone is the writer's soul. When Stephen Crane wrote, "The waves were barbarous and abrupt", he presented simultaneously the sea and the small boat. Waves are not abrupt for a ship. "Barbarous and abrupt"—onomatopoeic, like "Poluphloisboion" in Homer (when the Cyclops throws the rock).

Pound: (Concluding) How many have kept their promises since the *English Review* was founded twenty-five years ago?

Ford: Stephen Reynolds is dead. Ezra has become hangman's assistant to interviewers . . . I don't know what Wyndham Lewis is doing. Norman Douglas. D. H. Lawrence is dead, but kept on 'till the end. Rebecca West. Among the successors: Virginia Woolf; Joyce in "The Portrait of the Artist as a Young Man"; the Hughes who wrote "High Wind in Jamaica", a dramatist's novel, not a novel writer's.

EDITOR'S NOTE: (Above) From the original interview in Italian, appearing in "Il Mare" of Rapallo at the time of one of Ford's visits. Pestered the next day as to what a young writer ought to read, Ford groaned: "Let him get a DICTIONARY and learn the meaning of words."

A MATTER OF MODESTY

A MATTER OF MODESTY [1]

HAZ anybody here seen BANKHEAD? An nif not, who told him to hide? Bet it wasn't Tallulah!

"Virgin huntress chaste and fair"

or however that beautiful poEM runs. I bet it wasn't Tallulah tole ole pop, or ole Uncle John from Jasper fer to go hide in the bayou. That a man anna SenAtor from Allybarmer shd/have an idea, or shd/emit an idea before it wuz worn out and chucked in the dust-bin is NOOZ to the rest of the continent (European and Asiatic papers please copy, cause the Paris Press club was never TOLD).

Well, of course the poetry that gets printed, and the rich and rare caviar, not to say reparteee that is stored in the CONgressional record, will surprise future Babylonian researchists and bollygizers in the year UmTumUmptywufgle. But speaking of Bankhead, and his sidekick the revered Pettengill (a fish-like sort of a name), what they wishsper, I mean the learned gentry that have Purrfesser in front of their names and X.C.B., Dr. Xot. P.B. and so forth trailin', IZ "we don't think there is anyone here that will touch it, but we (plural, notice the plural) are very glad that you are (A R E , present tense) going ON Wiff it."

[1] In *Esquire* May, 1935.

"Does the senator ever eat?" said Senator Bankhead to a bone-headed colleague, speaking in the third person, as is formal.

What I am getting at is that, while fat Herbie was still in the Hite Whouse, an idea got into the Senate. I don't say it got in very far, or that Bankhead knew much about it. But still: EF evvury aMURikun citterzen had 30 cents in the morning thet he hadder spend before nex Choosdy night?

Of course that spells trade revival. And of course taxes iz all bloody hooey. I'ma TELLIN' you TAXES IZ nuts. There is no god damn use of TAXES. And there are more'n one way of doin' without 'em. Just the same as bright lads can git over the Ocean, the Atterlantic Oceam both by Zepperlin and by Air-plaine if they're good enough. Taxes IZ just plain baloney. Douglas tells you how to get rid of 'em. But it takes human intelligence to understand him, so it'z NO use to the Electorate.

And Sil Gesell put most of 'em onto MONEY. Heck! I say you can get taxes OFF what you eat, and shift the tax onto MONEY.

Doug don't like it, cause he says it za TAX. But if there wuzza tax on money onct a month, of one cent on the dollar it couldn't fall on anybody that didn't HAVE the dollar when it fall'd DUE. And that is damn near AXiomatic.

And there is no more reason for a country not paying its expenses in stamp-scrip than there is of my trying to borrow YOUR FEET to walk on.

Money is mostly now made out of paper, covered with print or engraving, with an occasional siggychoor.

And what the hell can it cost you to live? What can it COST the nation from one year's end to another? It costs what the nation uses up and wears out and chucks overboard.

And whatever import taxes IZ levied is paid by blokes INSide the country. And don't yew fergit it.

Mr. Keynes is written a book on the ballet. The ex-rhooshun ballet. The British ain't gawt nothin' on us. They got McDonald and Simon, so they got no right ter lafft at America. And as fer their kneeconymists. Well there's the ballet. Prof. Pigou, that used to explain to 'em Asquiff, has taken to Alpinism, and says he dun't care a pig's whistle. Which is wise of him at his age. And he is two jumps ahead of the American Univursteries that used to lap up his opinyums.

Lemme tell you again about the economists of the period. As Remy used to say: at Carneval time there is also "le costume historique," fancy clothes for the carneval or costume of the period, as Hem. said the dazzle orficer's clothes wuz.

An lemme tell you again, when Doug' sez to Llard Geo.'s frien' the "economist consulted of nations," he sez

"Wot is the cause of the H(igh) C(ost) of L(ivin'). The kneeconymist sez: "Lack of labour."

An' there wuz two millyum men out of work, in London town while he wuz sayin' it.

That, m' deerly beluffit bruddrem, is ECONOMICS as wuz, and hellass, as iz still taught in the kawledges. And there's a bloke called Von Mice in Geneva, fillin' up fewchoor Murkn deeplomat's with just that SAME sort of damn hooey and the pore young things wastin' time an' money to learn it, if they ain't there at the govvymint's charge.

An' how come Doug wuz in THAT gallery? Cause I took him, thass how he got there, plus SOCIAL pressure. I won't call her the "daughter of an hundred earls," 'cause Tennyson's joke about that "syndicate de paternite" never did seem to me in good taste. But at any rate she wuz might. And so I brought 'em together. AND it was worth it, ust like when I took Parson Elyot to see the Prima Ballerina and it evoked "Grushkin"; as you can see in that bewteeful poEM entytled "Whispers of Immortality."

So nobuddy can say I ain't done my bit fer science an' kulchur. Social xxxperiment. That's my methord. You have to go round and see things. The guvvyment could pay its expenses in stamp-scrip which eats up its own tail, and is easier to unnerstan' than brother Douglas (the great Scotch mahatma). But Doug's got the better HOW. Oh yes, when you folks get bright enough you will SEE that. But in the mean time. Fer something to use in normal (I don't think they are) but still, fer to get the idea . . . into motion. I think you better pay divvys in stamp scrip. Just to get used to the idEA thet the country HAS credit.

Like I don't go to a bank and borrow money, when I want to eat at my Albergo. Cause I got CREDIT. So has the nation got credit. And why the HELL don't we USE it? Cause you blokes don't KNOW that we got it. That's why we don't use it.

And the mos' discouragin' thing about the Administration has just been printed by Uppie Sinclair. Ghees!! wotter book he has written! "What a kind man," he sez. "What a luvvable man!" he sez. And he tells deh WOIL' wotter luvvybl man is the President, and inna few weeks he is out yellin: "His bassarly friens double X'd me!!"

But thet ain't the harf ov it deerie, what is DEEpressin' (Are we ter beeleev' it? I hope not) but WOT iz depressin' is Upton's story of how he wandered all about and around in them orfices down thaaar by the POtomack, and everybody listen'd to Upton, and everybody said "Yes, Sir," to Upton, and treated him as a light of intelligence. That bloke is no MONOmaniac. We gotter make a noo word fer Upton. Cause every notion that ever got into hiz bellfry iz nailed to the wall. If you get me. A Polymaniac, thass what is Upton. Every gordamn dead plastered notion that ever got into Upton has been shot, stuffed, mounted, an' put on the wall or the mantlepiece. His mind izza REAL muZEEum. And all the country needs, apart from a little good charwin'

terbakker, is fer Sis Perkins and a few more of Upton's
spiritual relations, to be appointed curators.

EZ P'O

or with my full siggychoor,

EZRA

GENESIS
or, The First Book In The Bible

GENESIS
or, *The First Book In The Bible* [1]

("SUBJECT TO AUTHORITY")

T HE sacred author of this work, Genesis, complied with the ideas acceptable to his era; it was almost necessary; for without this condescension he would not have been understood. There remain for us merely a few reflections on the physics of those remote times. As for the theology of the book: we respect it, we believe it most firmly, we would not risk the faintest touch to its surface.

"In the beginning God created heaven and earth." That is the way they translate it, yet there is scarcely any one so ignorant as not to know that the original reads "the gods created heaven and earth"; which reading conforms to the Phœnician idea that God employed lesser divinities to untangle chaos. The Phœnicians had been long established when the Hebrews broke into some few provinces of their land. It was quite natural that these latter should have learned their language and borrowed their ideas of the cosmos.

Did the ancient Phœnician philosophers in "the time of Moses" know enough to regard the earth as a point in relation to the multitude of globes which God has placed in immensity? The very ancient and false idea

[1] Translated from an eighteenth-century author.

167

that heaven was made for the earth has nearly always prevailed among ignorant peoples. It is scarcely possible that such good navigators as the Phœnicians should not have had a few decent astronomers, but the old prejudices were quite strong, and were gently handled by the author of Genesis, who wrote to teach us God's ways and not to instruct us in physics.

"The earth was all *tohu bohu* and void, darkness was over the face of the deep, the spirit of God was borne on the waters."

"Tohu bohu" means precisely chaos, disorder. The earth was not yet formed as it is at present. Matter existed, the divine power had only to straighten things out. The "spirit of God" is literally the "breath" or "wind" which stirred up the waters. This idea is found in fragments of the Phœnician author, Sanchoniathon. The Phœnicians, like all the other peoples of antiquity, believed matter eternal. There is not one author of all those times who ever said that one could make something of nothing. Even in the Bible there is no passage which claims that matter was made out of nothing, not but what this creation from nothing is true, but its verity was unknown to the carnal Jews.

Men have been always divided on the eternity of the world, but never on the eternity of matter.

"*Gigni de nihilo nihilum, et in nihilum nil posse reverti,*" writes Persius, and all antiquity shared his opinion. God said, "Let there be light," and there was light, and he saw that the light was good, and he divided the light from darkness, and he called the light *day* and the darkness *night,* and this was the evening and the morning of the first day. And God also said that the firmament, etc., the second day . . . saw that it was good.

Let us begin by seeing whether the bishop of Avranches Huet, Leclerc, etc., are right, against those who claim that this is a sublime piece of eloquence.

The Jewish author lumps in the light with the other objects of creation; he uses the same turn of phrase, "saw that it was good." The sublime should lift itself above the average. Light is no better treated than anything else in this passage. It was another respected opinion that light did not come from the sun. Men saw it spread through the air before sunrise and after sunset; they thought the sun served merely to reinforce it. The author of Genesis conforms to popular error: he has the sun and moon made four days after the light. It is unlikely that there was a morning and evening before the sun came into being, but the inspired author bows to the vague and stupid prejudice of his nation. It seems probable that God was not attempting to educate the Jews in philosophy or cosmogony. He could lift their spirits straight into truth, *but* he *preferred* to descend to their level. One can not repeat this answer too often.

The separation of the light from the darkness is not part of another physical theory; it seems that night and day were mixed up like two kinds of grain; and that they were sifted out of each other. It is sufficiently well established that darkness is nothing but the deprivation of light, and that there is light only in so far as our eyes receive the sensation, but no one had thought of this at that time.

The idea of the firmament is also of respectable antiquity. People imagined the skies very solid, because the same set of things always happened there. The skies circulated over our heads, they must therefore be very strong. The means of calculating how many exhalations of the earth and how many seas would be needed to keep the clouds full of water? There was then no Halley to write out the equations. There were tanks of water in heaven. These tanks were held up on a good steady dome; but one could see through the dome; it must have been made out of crystal. In order that the water could be poured over the earth there had to be doors, sluices, cataracts which could be opened, turned on. Such was the current astronomy, *and* one was writing for Jews; it was quite necessary to take up their silly ideas, which they had borrowed from other peoples only a little less stupid.

"God made two great lights, one to preside over the day, the other the night, and he made also the stars."

True, this shows the same continuous ignorance of nature. The Jews did not know that the moonlight is merely reflection. The author speaks of the stars as luminous points, which they look like, although they are at times suns with planets swinging about them. But holy spirit harmonized with the mind of the time. If he had said that the sun is a million times as large as the earth, and the moon fifty times smaller, no one would have understood him. They appear to be two stars of sizes not very unequal.

"God said also: let us make man in our image, let him rule over the fishes, etc."

What did the Jews mean by "in our image"? They meant, like all antiquity:

Finxit in effigiem moderantum cuncta deorum.

One can not make "images" save of bodies. No nation then imagined a bodiless god, and it is impossible to picture him as such. One might indeed say "god is nothing of anything we know," but then one would not have any idea what he is. The Jews constantly believed god corporal, as did all the rest of the nations. All the first fathers of the church also believed god corporal, until they had swallowed Plato's ideas, or rather until the lights of Christianity had grown purer.

"He created them male and female."

If God or the secondary gods created man male and female in their resemblance, it would seem that the Jews

believed God and the Gods were male and female. One
searches to see whether the author meant to say that man
was at the start ambisextrous or if he means that God
made Adam and Eve the same day. The most natural
interpretation would be that god made Adam and Eve
at the same time, but this is absolutely contradicted by
the formation of woman from the rib, a long time after
the first seven days.

"And he rested the seventh day."

The Phœnicians, Chaldeans, and Indians say that God
made the world in six periods, which Zoroaster calls the
six gahambars, as celebrated among Persians.

It is incontestable that all these people had a theogony
long before the Jews got to Horeb and Sinai, and before
they could have had writers. Several savants think it
likely that the allegory of the six days is imitated from
the six periods. God might have permitted great nations to have this idea before he inspired the Jews, just
as he had permitted other people to discover the arts
before the Jews had attained any.

"The place of delight shall be a river which waters a
garden, and from it shall flow four rivers, Phison . . .
Gehon . . ., etc., Tigris, Euphrates . . ."

According to this version the terrestrial paradise would
have contained about a third of Asia and Africa. The
Euphrates and Tigris have their sources sixty miles apart
in hideous mountains which do not look the least like a
garden. The river which borders Ethiopia can be only
the Nile, whose source is a little over a thousand miles
from those of the Tigris and the Euphrates; and if Phison is the Phase, it is curious to start a Scythian river
from the fount of a river of Africa. One must look
further afield for the meaning of all these rivers. Every
commentator makes his own Eden.

Some one has said that the Garden was like the gardens of Eden at Saana in Arabia Felix celebrated in antiquity, and that the parvenu Hebrews might have been an Arab tribe taking to themselves credit for the prettiest thing in the best canton of Arabia, as they have always taken to themselves the traditions of all the great peoples who enslaved them. But in any case they were led by the Lord.

"The Lord took man and set him in the midst of the garden, to tend it." It was all very well saying "tend it," "cultivate the garden," but it would have been very difficult for Adam to cultivate a garden 3,000 miles long. Perhaps he had helpers. It is another chance for the commentators to exercise their gifts of divination . . . as they do with the rivers.

"Eat not of the fruit of the knowledge of good and evil." It is difficult to think that there was a tree which taught good and evil; as there are pear trees and peach trees. One asks why God did not wish man to know good from evil. Would not the opposite wish (if one dare say so) appear more worthy of God, and much more needful to man? It seems to our poor reason that God might have ordered him to eat a good deal of this fruit, but one must submit one's reason and conclude that obedience to God is the proper course for us.

"If you eat of the fruit you shall die."

Yet Adam ate, and did not die in the least; they say he lived another nine centuries. Several "Fathers" have considered all this as an allegory. Indeed, one may say that other animals do not know that they die, but that man knows it through his reason. This reason is the tree of knowledge which makes him foresee his finish. This explanation may be more reasonable, but we do not dare to pronounce on it.

"The Lord said also: It is not good that man should be alone, let us make him an helpmate like to him." One expects that the Lord is going to give him a woman, but first he brings up all the beasts. This may be the transposition of some copyist.

"And the name which Adam gave to each animal is its real name." An animal's real name would be one which designated all the qualifications of its species, or at least the principal traits, but this does not exist in any language. There are certain imitative words, cock and cuckoo, and *alali* in Greek, etc. Moreover, if Adam had known the real names and therefore the properties of the animals, he must have already eaten of the tree of knowledge; or else it would seem that God need not have forbidden him the tree, since he already knew more than the Royal Society, or the Academy.

Observe that this is the first time Adam is named in Genesis. The first man according to the Brahmins was Adimo, son of the earth. Adam and Eve mean the same thing in Phœnician, another indication that the holy spirit fell in with the received ideas.

"When Adam was asleep, etc., . . . rib . . . made a woman." The Lord, in the preceding chapter, had already created them male and female; why should he take a rib out of the man to make a woman already existing? We are told that the author announces in one place what he explains in another. We are told that this allegory shows woman submitted to her husband. Many people have believed on the strength of these verses that men have one rib less than women, but this is an heresy and anatomy shows us that a woman is no better provided with ribs than her husband.

"Now the serpent was the most subtle of beasts," etc., "he said to the woman," etc.

There is nowhere the least mention of the devil or a devil. All is physical. The serpent was considered not only the subtlest of all beasts by all oriental nations; he was also believed immortal. The Chaldeans had a fable about a fight between God and a serpent; it is preserved by Pherecides. Origen cites it in his sixth book against Celsus. They carried snakes in the feasts of Bacchus. The Egyptians attributed a sort of divinity to the serpent, as Eusebius tells us in his "Evangelical Preparations," book I, chapter X. In India and Arabia, and in China, the serpent was the symbol of life; the Chinese emperors before Moses wore the serpent sign on their breasts.

Eve is not surprised at the serpent's talking to her. Animals are always talking in the old stories; thus when Pilpai and Locman make animals talk no one is ever surprised.

All this tale seems physical and denuded of allegory. It even tells us the reason why the serpent who ramped before this now crawls on its belly, and why we always try to destroy it (at least so they say); precisely as we are told in all ancient metamorphoses why the crow, who was white, is now black, why the owl stays at home in the daytime, etc. But the "Fathers" have believed it an allegory manifest and respectable, and it is safest to believe them.

"I will multiply your griefs and your pregnancies, ye shall bring forth children with grief, ye shall be beneath the power of the man and he shall rule over you." One asks why the multiplication of pregnancies is a punishment. It was on the contrary a very great blessing, and especially for the Jews. The pains of childbirth are alarming only for delicate women; those accustomed to work are brought to bed very easily, especially in hot climates. On the other hand, animals sometimes suffer in littering, and even die of it. As for the superiority of man over woman, this is the quite natural result of his bodily and intellectual forces. The male organs are generally more capable of consecutive effort, more fit for manual and intellectual tasks. But when the woman has fist or wit stronger than those of her husband she rules the roost, and the man is submitted to woman. This is true, *but* before the original sin there may have been neither pain nor submission.

"God made them tunics of skin."

This passage proves very nicely that the Jews believed in a corporal god. A Rabbi named Eliezer has written that God covered Adam and Eve with the skin of the tempter serpent; Origen claims that the "tunic of skin" was a new flesh, a new body which God made for man, but one should have more respect for the text.

"And the Lord said 'Behold Adam, who is become like one of us.'" It seems that the Jews at first admired several gods. It is considerably more difficult to make out what they mean by the word God, *Eloim*. Several commentators state that this phrase, "one of us," means the Trinity, but there is no question of the Trinity in the Bible.[1]

The Trinity is not a composite of several gods, it is the same god tripled; the Jews never heard tell of a god in three persons. By these words "like unto us" it is probable that the Jews meant angels, Eloïm. For this reason various rash men of learning have thought that the book was not written until a time when the Jews had adopted a belief in inferior gods, but this view is condemned.[2]

"The Lord set him outside the garden of delights, that he might dig in the earth." Yet some say that God had put him in the garden, in order that he might cultivate *it*. If gardener Adam merely became laborer Adam, he was not so much the worse off. This solution of the diffi-

[1] The reader will remember in Landor's Chinese dialogues, when the returned mandarin is telling the Emperor's children about England, there is one place where they burst into giggles "because they had been taught some arithmetic."

[2] The reader is referred to our heading: "Subject to authority."

culty does not seem to us sufficiently serious. It would
be better to say that God punished Adam's disobedience
by banishing him from his birthplace.

Certain over-temerarious commentators say that the
whole of the story refers to an idea once common to all
men, i.e., that past times were better than present. People have always bragged of the past in order to run down
the present. Men overburdened with work have imagined that pleasure is idleness, not having had wit enough
to conceive that man is never worse off than when he has
nothing to do. Men seeing themselves not infrequently
miserable forged an idea of a time when all men were
happy. It is as if they had said, once upon a time no tree
withered, no beast fell sick, no animal devoured another,
the spiders did not catch flies. Hence the ideal of the
Golden Age, of the egg of Arimana, of the serpent who
stole the secret of eternal life from the donkey, of the
combat of Typhon and Osiris, of Ophionée and the gods,
of Pandora's casket, and all these other old stories, sometimes very ingenious and never, in the least way, instruc-
tive. *But* we should believe that the fables of other nations are imitation of Hebrew history, since we still have
the Hebrew history and the history of other savage peoples is for the most part destroyed. Moreover, the wit-
nesses in favor of Genesis are quite irrefutable.

"And he set before the garden of delight a cherubin
with a turning and flaming sword to keep guard over the
gateway to the tree of life." The word "kerub" means
bullock. A bullock with a burning sword is an odd sight
at a doorway. But the Jews have represented angels as
bulls and as sparrow hawks, despite the prohibition to
make graven images. Obviously they got these bulls and
hawks from Egyptians who imitated all sorts of things,
and who worshipped the bull as the symbol of agriculture and the hawk as the symbol of winds. Probably the
tale is an allegory, a Jewish allegory, the kerub means

"nature." A symbol made of a bull's body, a man's head and a hawk's wings.

"The Lord put his mark upon Cain."

"What a Lord!" say the incredulous. He accepts Abel's offering, rejects that of the elder brother, without giving any trace of a reason. The Lord provided the cause of the first brotherly enmity. This is a moral instruction, most truly, a lesson to be learned from all ancient fables, to wit, that scarcely had the race come into existence before one brother assassinated another, but what appears to the wise of this world, contrary to all justice, contrary to all the common sense principles, is that God has eternally damned the whole human race, and has slaughtered his own son, quite uselessly, for an apple, and that he has pardoned a fratricide. Did I say "pardoned"? He takes the criminal under his own protection. He declares that any one who avenges the murder of Abel shall be punished with seven fold the punishment inflicted on Cain. He puts on him his sign as a safeguard. The impious call the story both execrable and absurd. It is the delirium of some unfortunate Israelite, who wrote these inept infamies in imitation of stories so abundant among the neighboring Syrians. This insensate Hebrew attributed his atrocious invention to Moses, at a time when nothing was rarer than books. Destiny, which disposes of all things, has preserved his work till our day; scoundrels have praised it, and idiots have believed. Thus say the horde of theists, who while adoring God, have been so rash as to condemn the Lord God of Israel, and who judge the actions of the Eternal Being by the rules of our imperfect ethics, and our erroneous justice. They admit a god but submit god to our laws. Let us guard against such temerity, and let us once again learn to respect what lies beyond our compre-

hension. Let us cry out "O Altitudo!" with all our
strength.

"The Gods, Eloïm, seeing that the daughters of men
were fair, took for spouses those whom they chose."
This flight of imagination is also common to all the nations. There is no race, except perhaps the Chinese,[1]

I am unable to make out whether the girl is more than a
priestess. She bathes in hot water made fragrant by boiling
orchids in it, she washes her hair and binds iris into it, she
puts on the dress of flowery colors, and the god illimitable in
his brilliance descends: she continues her attention to her
toilet, in very reverent manner.   P.

which has not recorded gods getting young girls with
child. Corporeal gods come down to look at their do-
main, they see our young ladies and take the best for
themselves; children produced in this way are better
than other folks' children; thus Genesis does not omit to
say that this commerce bred giants. Once again the book
is in key with vulgar opinion.

"And I will pour the water floods over the earth."

I would note here that St. Augustin (City of God, No.
8) says, "*Maximum illud diluvium graeca nec latina novit
historia.*" Neither Greek nor Latin history takes note of
this very great flood. In truth, they knew only Deu-
calion's and Ogyges' in Greece. These were regarded as
universal in the fables collected by Ovid, but were totally
unknown in Eastern Asia. St. Augustin is not in error
when he says history makes no mention thereof.

"God said to Noah: I will make an agreement with
you and with your seed after you, and with all the animals." God make an agreement with animals! The unbelievers will exclaim: "What a contract!" But if he

[1] In Fenollosa's notes on Kutsugen's ode to "Sir in the Clouds,"

make an alliance with man, why not with the animals?
What nice feeling, there is something quite as divine in
this sentiment as in the most metaphysical thought.
Moreover, animals feel better than most men think. It
is apparently in virtue of this agreement that St. Francis
of Assisi, the founder of the seraphic order, said to the
grasshoppers, and hares, "Sing, sister hoppergrass, brouse
brother rabbit." But what were the terms of the treaty?
That all the animals should devour each other; that they
should live on our flesh; and we on theirs; that after having eaten all we can we should exterminate all the rest,
and that we should only omit the devouring of men
strangled with our own hands. If there was any such pact
it was presumably made with the devil.

Probably this passage is only intended to show that
God is in equal degree master of all things that breathe.
This pact could only have been a command; it is called
"alliance" merely by an "extension of the word's meaning." One should not quibble over mere terminology,
but worship the spirit, and go back to the time when they
wrote this work which is scandal to the weak, but quite
edifying to the strong.

"And I will put my bow in the sky, and it shall be a
sign of our pact." Note that the author does not say
"I have put" but "I will put my bow"; this shows that
in common opinion the bow had not always existed. It
is a phenomenon of necessity caused by the rain, and
they give it as a supernatural manifestation that the
world shall never more be covered with water. It is odd
that they should choose a sign of rain as a promise that
one shall not be drowned. But one may reply to this:
when in danger of inundations we may be reassured by
seeing a rainbow.

"Now the Lord went down to see the city which the
children of Adam had builded, and he said, behold a
people with only one speech. They have begun this
and won't quit until it is finished. Let us go down and

confound their language, so that no man may understand his neighbor." Note merely that the sacred author still conforms to vulgar opinion. He always speaks of God as of a man who informs himself of what is going on, who wants to see with his eyes what is being done on his estate, and who calls his people together to determine a course of action.

"And Abraham, having arrayed his people (there were of them three hundred and eighteen), fell upon the five kings and slew them and pursued them even to Hoba on the left side of Damas." From the south side of the lake of Sodom to Damas is 24 leagues, and they still had to cross Liban and anti-Liban. Unbelievers exult over such tremendous exaggeration. But since the Lord favored Abraham there is *no* exaggeration.

"And that evening two angels came into Sodom, etc." The history of the two angels whom the Sodomites wanted to ravish is perhaps the most extraordinary which antiquity has produced. But we must remember that all Asia believed in incubi and succubæ demons, and that moreover these angels were creatures more perfect than man, and that they were probably much better looking, and lit more desires in a jaded, corrupt race than common men would have excited. Perhaps this part of the story is only a figure of rhetoric to express the horrible lewdness of Sodom and of Gomorrah. We offer this solution to savants with the most profound self-mistrust.

As for Lot who offered his two daughters to the Sodomites in lieu of the angels, and Lot's wife metamorphosed into the saline image, and all the rest of the story, what can one say of it? The ancient fable of Cinyra and Myrrha has some relation to Lot's incest with his daughters, the adventure of Philemon and Baucis is not without its points of comparison with that of the two angels appearing to Lot and his wife. As for the pillar of salt, I do not know what it compares with, perhaps with the story of Orpheus and Eurydice?

A number of savants think with Newton and the learned Leclerc that the Pentateuch was written by Samuel when the Jews had learned reading and writing, and that all these tales are imitation of Syrian fable.

But it is sufficient for us that it is all Holy Scripture; we therefore revere it without searching in it for anything that is not the work of the Holy Spirit. We should remember, at all times, that these times are not our times, and we should not fail to add our word to that of so many great men who have declared that the Old Testament is true history, and that everything invented by all the rest of the universe is mere fable.

Some savants have pretended that one should remove from the canonical books all incredible matters which might be a stumbling block to the feeble, but it is said that these savants were men of corrupt heart and that they ought to be burned, and that it is impossible to be an honest man unless you believe that the Sodomites desired to ravish the angels. This is the reasoning of a species of monster who wishes to rule over wits.

It is true that several celebrated church fathers have had the prudence to turn all these tales into allegory, like the Jews, and Philo in especial. Popes still more prudent desired to prevent the translation of these books into the everyday tongue, for fear men should be led to pass judgment on what was upheld for their adoration.

One ought surely to conclude that those who perfectly understand this work should tolerate those who do not understand it, for if these latter do not understand it, it is not their fault; also those who do not understand it should tolerate those who understand it most fully.

Savants, too full of their knowledge, have claimed that Moses could not possibly have written the book of Genesis. One of their reasons is that in the story of

Abraham, the patriarch pays for his wife's funeral plot in coined money, and that the king of Gerare gives a thousand pieces of silver to Sarah when he returns her, after having stolen her for her beauty in the seventy-fifth year of her age. They say that, having consulted authorities, they find that there was no coined money in those days. But it is quite clear that this is pure chicane on their part, since the Church has always believed most firmly that Moses did write the Pentateuch. They strengthen all the doubts raised by the disciples of Aben-Hesra and Baruch Spinoza. The physician Astruc, father-in-law of the comptroller-general Silhouette, in his book, now very rare, entitled "Conjectures on Genesis," adds new objections, unsolvable to human wisdom; but not to humble submissive piety. The savants dare to contradict every line, the simple revere every line. Guard against falling into the misfortune of trusting our human reason, be contrite in heart and in spirit.

"And Abraham said that Sarah was his sister, and the king of Gerare took her to him." We confess, as we have said in our essay on Abraham, that Sarah was then ninety years old; that she had already been kidnapped by one King of Egypt; and that a king of this same desert Gerare later kidnapped the wife of Abraham's son Isaac. We have also spoken of the servant Agar, by whom Abraham had a son, and of how Abraham treated them both. One knows what delight unbelievers take in these stories; with what supercilious smiles they consider them; how they set the story of Abimelech and this same wife of Abraham's (Sarah) whom he passed off as his sister, above the "1001 nights" and also that of another Abimelech in love with Rebecca, whom Isaac also passed off as his sister. One can not too often reiterate that the fault of all these studious critics lies in their persistent endeavour to bring all these things into accord with our feeble reason and to judge ancient Arabs as they would judge the French court or the English.

"The soul of Sichem, son of King Hemor, cleaved to the soul of Dinah, and he charmed his sadness with her tender caresses, and he went to Hemor his father, and said unto him: Give me this woman for wife." Here the savants are even more refractory. What! a king's son marry a vagabond's daughter. Jacob her father loaded with presents! The king receives into his city these wandering robbers, called patriarchs; he has the incredible and incomprehensible kindness to get himself circumcised, he and his son, his court and his people, in order to condescend to the superstition of this little tribe which did not own a half league of land! And what reward do our holy patriarchs make him for such astonishing kindness? They wait the day when the wound of circumcision ordinarily produces a fever. Then Simeon and Levi run throughout the city, daggers in hand; they massacre the king, the prince, his son, and all the inhabitants. The horror of this St. Bartholomew is only diminished by its impossibility. It is a shocking romance but it is obviously a ridiculous romance: It is impossible that two men could have killed a whole nation. One might suffer some inconvenience from one's excerpted foreskin, but one would defend oneself against two scoundrels, one would assemble, surround them, finish them off as they deserved.

But there is one more impossible statement: by an exact supputation of date, we find that Dinah, daughter of Jacob, was at this time no more than three years of age; even if one tries to accommodate the chronology, she could not have been more than five: it is this that causes complaint. People say: What sort of a book is this? The book of a reprobate people, a book for so long unknown to all the earth, a book where right, reason and decent custom are outraged on every page, and which we have presented us as irrefutable, holy, dictated by God himself? Is it not an impiety to believe it? Is it not the dementia of cannibals to persecute sensible, modest men who do not believe it?

To which we reply: The Church says she believes it. Copyists may have introduced revolting absurdities into reverend stories. Only the Holy Church can be judge of such matters. The profane should be led by her wisdom. These absurdities, these pretended horrors do not affect the basis of our religion. Where would men be if the cult of virtue depended on what happened long ago to Sichem and little Dinah?

"Behold the Kings who reigned in the land of Edom, before the children of Israel had a king."

Behold another famous passage, another stone which doth hinder our feet. It is this passage which determined the great Newton, the pious and sage Samuel Clarke, the deeply philosophical Bolingbroke, the learned Leclerc, the savant Fréret, and a great number of other scholars to argue that Moses could not have been the author of Genesis.

We do indeed confess that these words could only have been written at a time when the Jews had kings.

It is chiefly this verse which determined Astruc to upset the whole book of Genesis, and to hypothecate memories on which the real author had drawn. His work is ingenious, exact, but rash. A council would scarcely have dared to undertake it. And to what end has it served, this ungrateful, dangerous work of this Astruc? To redouble the darkness which he set out to enlighten. This is ever the fruit of that tree of knowledge whereof we all wish to eat. Why should it be necessary that the fruits of the tree of ignorance should be more nourishing and more easy to manage?

But what matter to us, after all, whether this verse, or this chapter, was written by Moses, or by Samuel or by the priest from Samaria, or by Esdras, or by any one else? In what way can our government, our laws, our fortunes, our morals, our well being, be tied up with the ignorant chiefs of an unfortunate barbarous country, called Edom or Idumea, always peopled by thieves? Alas, these poor shirtless Arabs never ask about our existence, they pillage caravans and eat barley bread, and we torment ourselves trying to find out whether there were kinglets in one canton of Arabia Petra before they appeared in the neighboring canton to the west of lake Sodom.

O miseras hominium mentes! O pectora caeca! [1]

[1] Our author's treatment of Ezekiel merits equal attention. The illiteracy of literary circles or of *Little Review* readers may be indicated by the fact that no critic recognized the source of this skit (Voltaire). One reviewer complained of my digging up the Baron Holbach.

OUR TETRARCHAL
PRÉCIEUSE

OUR TETRARCHAL
PRÉCIEUSE

(A DIVAGATION FROM JULES LAFORGUE)

There arose, as from a great ossified sponge, the comic-opera, Florence-Nightingale light-house, with junks beneath it clicking in vesperal, meretricious monotony; behind them the great cliff obtruded solitary into the oily, poluphloisbious ocean, lifting its confection of pylons; the poplar rows, sunk yards, Luna Parks, etc., of the Tetrarchal Palace polished jasper and basalt, funereal, undertakerial, lugubrious, blistering in the high-lights under a pale esoteric sun-beat; encrusted, bespattered and damascened with cynocephali, sphinxes, winged bulls, bulbuls, and other sculptural by-laws. The screech-owls from the jungle could only look out upon the shadowed parts of the sea, which they did without optic inconvenience, so deep was the obscured contagion of their afforested blackness.

The two extraneous princes went up toward the stable-yard, gaped at the effulgence of peacocks, glared at the derisive gestures of the horse-cleaners, adumbrated insults, sought vainly for a footman or any one to take up their cards.

The tetrarch appeared on a terrace, removing his ceremonial gloves.

The water, sprinkled in the streets in anticipation of the day's parade, dried in little circles of dust. The tetrarch puffed at his hookah with an exaggeration of

189

dignity; he was disturbed at the presence of princes, he was disturbed by the presence of Jao; he desired to observe his own ruin, the slow deliquescence of his position, with a fitting detachment and lassitude. Jao had distributed pamphlets, the language was incomprehensible; Jao had been stored in the cellarage, his following distributed pamphlets.

In the twentieth century of his era the house of Emeraud Archytypas was about to have its prize bit of fireworks: a war with the other world . . . after so many ages of purely esoteric culture!

Jao had declined both the poisoned coffee and the sacred sword of the Samurai, courtesies offered, in this case, to an incomprehensible foreigner. Even now, with a superlation of form, the sacred kriss had been sent to the court executioner, it was no mere every-day implement. The princes arrived at this juncture. There sounded from the back alleys the preparatory chirping of choral societies, and the wailing of pink-lemonade sellers. To-morrow the galley would be gone.

Leaning over the syrupy clematis, Emeraud crumbled brioches for the fishes, reminding himself that he had not yet collected the remains of his wits. There was no galvanization known to art, science, industry or the ministrations of sister-souls that would rouse his long since respectable carcass.

Yet at his birth a great tempest had burst above the dynastic manor; credible persons had noticed the lightnings scrolling Alpha and Omega above it; and nothing had happened. He had given up flagellation. He walked daily to the family necropolis: a cool place in the summer. He summoned the Arranger of Inanities.

2.

Strapped, pomaded, gloved, laced; with patulous beards, with their hair parted at the backs of their heads;

with their cork-screw curls pulled back from their foreheads to give themselves tone on their medallions; with
helmets against one hip; twirling the musk-balls of their
sabres with their disengaged restless fingers, the hyper-
borean royalties were admitted. And the great people
received them, in due order: chief mandarins in clump,
the librarian of the palace (Conde de las Navas), the
Arbiter Elegantium, the Curator major of Symbols, the
Examiner of the High Schools, the Supernumerary priest
of the Snow Cult, the Administrator of Death, and the
Chief Attendant Collector of Death-duties.

Their Highnesses bowed and addressed the Tetrarch:
". . . felicitous wind . . . day so excessively glorious
. . . wafted . . . these isles . . . notwithstanding not
also whereof . . . basilica far exceeding . . . Ind, Or-
mus . . . Miltonesco . . . etc. . . . to say nothing of
the seven-stopped barbary organ and the Tedium lauda-
mus . . . etc. . . ."

(Lunch was brought in.)

Kallipagous artichokes, a light collation of tunny-fish,
asparagus served on pink reeds, eels pearl-gray and dove-
gray, gamut and series of compôtes and various wines
(without alcohol).

Under impulsion of the Arranger of Inanities the
pomaded princes next began their inspection of the
buildings. A pneumatic lift hove them upward to the
outer rooms of Salome's suite. The lift door clicked on its
gilt-brass double expansion-clamps; the procession advanced between rows of wall-facing negresses whose
naked shoulder-blades shone like a bronze of oily opacity.
They entered the hall of majolica, very yellow with thick
blue incrustations, glazed images, with flushed and pro-
tuberant faces; in the third atrium they came upon a
basin of joined ivory, a white bath-sponge, rather large,
a pair of very pink slippers. The next room was littered
with books bound in white vellum and pink satin; the
next with mathematical instruments, hydrostats, sextants,

astrolabial discs, the model of a gasolene motor, a nickel-plated donkey engine. . . . They proceeded up metal stairs to the balcony, from which a rustling and swaying and melodiously enmousselined figure, jonquil-colored and delicate, preceded or rather predescended them by dumb-waiter, a route which they were not ready to follow. The machine worked for five floors: usage private and not ceremonial.

The pomaded princes stood to attention, bowed with deference and with gallantry. The Arranger ignored the whole incident, ascended the next flight of stairs and began on the telescope:

"Grand equatorial, 22 yards inner tube length, revolvable cupola (frescoes in water-tight paint) weight 200,089 kilos, circulating on fourteen steel castors in a groove of chloride of magnesium, 2 minutes for complete revolution. The princess can turn it herself."

The princes allowed their attention to wander, they noted their ship beneath in the harbor, and calculated the drop, they then compared themselves with the brocaded and depilated denizens of the escort, after which they felt safer. They were led passively into the Small Hall of Perfumes, presented with protochlorine of mercury, bismuth regenerators, cantharides, lustral waters guaranteed free from hydrated lead. Were conducted thence to the hanging garden, where the form hermetically enmousselined, the jonquil-colored gauze with the pea-sized dark spots on it, disappeared from the opposite slope. Molossian hounds yapping and romping about her.

The trees lifted their skinned-salmon trunks, the heavy blackness was broken with a steely, metallic sunshine. A sea wind purred through the elongated forest like an express-train in a tunnel. Polychrome statues obtruded themselves from odd corners. An elephant swayed absentmindedly, the zoo was loose all over the place. The keeper of the aquarium moralized for an hour upon the calm life of his fishes. From beneath the dark tanks the hareem sent up a decomposed odor, and a melancholy slave chantey saturated the corridors, a low droning osmosis. They advanced to the cemetery, wanting all the time to see Jao.

This exhibit came at last in its turn. They were let down in a sling-rope through a musty nitrated grill, observing in this descent the ill-starred European in his bath-robe, his nose in a great fatras of papers overscrawled with illegible pot-hooks.

He rose at their hefty salutation; readjusted his spectacles, blinked; and then it came over him: These damn pustulent princes! Here! and at last! Memory overwhelmed him. How many, on how many rotten December and November evenings had he stopped, had he not stopped in the drizzle, in the front line of workmen, his nose crushed against a policeman, and craning his scraggy neck to see *them* getting out of their state barouche, going up the interminable front stairway to the big-windowed rococo palace; he muttering that the "Times" were at hand.

And now the revolution was accomplished. The proletariat had deputed them. They were here to howk him out of quod; a magnificent action, a grace of royal humility, performed at the will of the people, the new era had come into being. He saluted them automatically, searching for some phrase European, historic, fraternal, of course, but still noble.

The Royal Nephew, an oldish military man with a bald-spot, ubiquitarian humorist, joking with every one in season and out (like Napoleon), hating all doctrinaires (like Napoleon), was however the first to break silence: "Huk, heh, old sour bean, bastard of Jean Jacques Rousseau, is *this* where you've come to be hanged? Eh? I'm damned if it ain't a good thing."

The unfortunate publicist stiffened.

"Idealogue!" said the Nephew.

The general strike had been unsuccessful. Jao bent with emotion. Tears showed in his watery eyes, slid down his worn cheek, trickled into his scraggy beard. There was then a sudden change in his attitude. He began to murmur caresses in the gentlest of European diminutives.

They started. There was a tinkle of keys, and through a small opposite doorway they discerned the last flash of the mousseline, the pale, jonquil-colored, blackspotted.

The Nephew readjusted his collar. A subdued cortège reascended.

3

The ivory orchestra lost itself in gay fatalistic improvisation; the opulence of two hundred over-fed tetrarchal Dining-Companions swished in the Evening salon, and overflowed coruscated couches. They slithered through their genuflections to the throne. The princes puffed out their elbows, simultaneously attempting to disentangle their Collars-of-the-Fleece in the idea that these would be a suitable present for their entertainer. Neither succeeded; suddenly in the midst of the so elaborate setting they perceived the æsthetic nullity of the ornament, its connotations were too complex to go into.

The tetrarchal children (superb productions, in the strictly esoteric sense) were led in over the jonquil-colored reed-matting. A water-jet shot up from the centre of the great table, and fell plashing above on the red and white rubber awning. A worn entertainment beset the diminutive music-hall stage: acrobats, flower-dancers, contortionists, comic wrestlers, to save the guests conversation. A trick skater was brought in on real ice, did the split, engraved a gothic cathedral. The Virgin Serpent as she was called, entered singing "Biblis,

Biblis"; she was followed by a symbolic Mask of the Graces; which gave place to trapeze virtuosi.

An horizontal geyser of petals was shot over the auditorium. The hookahs were brought in. Jao presumably heard all this over his head. The diners' talk became general, the princes supporting the army, authority, religion a bulwark of the state, international arbitration, the perfectibility of the race; the mandarins of the palace held for the neutralization of contacts, initiated cenacles, frugality and segregation.

The music alone carried on the esoteric undertone, silence spread with great feathers, poised hawk-wise. Salome appeared on the high landing, descended the twisted stair, still stiff in her sheath of mousseline; a small ebony lyre dangled by a gilt cord from her wrist; she nodded to her parent; paused before the Alcazar curtain, balancing, swaying on her anæmic pigeon-toed little feet—until every one had had a good look at her. She looked at no one in particular; her hair dusty with exiguous pollens curled down over her narrow shoulders, ruffled over her forehead, with stems of yellow flowers twisted into it. From the dorsal joist of her bodice, from a sort of pearl matrix socket there rose a peacock tail, moire, azure, glittering with shot emerald: an halo for her marble-white face.

Superior, graciously careless, conscious of her uniqueness, of her autochthonous entity, her head cocked to the left, her eyes fermented with the interplay of contradictory expiations, her lips a pale circonflex, her teeth with still paler gums showing their super-crucified half-smile. An exquisite recluse, formed in the island æsthetic, there alone comprehended. Hermetically enmousselined, the black spots in the fabric appeared so many punctures in the soft brightness of her sheath. Her arms of angelic nudity, the two breasts like two minute almonds, the scarf twined just above the adorable umbilical groove (nature desires that nude woman should be adorned with a girdle) composed in a cup-shaped embrace of the hips. Behind her the peacock halo, her pale pigeon-toed feet covered only by the watered-yellow fringe and by the bright-yellow anklet. She balanced, a little budding messiah; her head over-weighted; not knowing what to do with her hands; her petticoat so simple, art long, very long, and life so very inextensive; so obviously ready for the cosy-corner, for little talks in conservatories . . .

And she was going to speak . . .

The Tetrarch bulged in his cushions, as if she had already said something. His attention compelled that of the princes; he brushed aside the purveyor of pineapples.

She cleared her throat, laughing, as if not to be taken too seriously; the sexless, timbreless voicelet, like that of a sick child asking for medicine, began to the lyre accompaniment:

"Canaan, excellent nothingness; nothingness-latent, circumambient, about to be the day after to-morrow, incipient, estimable, absolving, coexistent . . ."

The princes were puzzled. "Concessions by the five senses to an all-inscribing affective insanity; latitudes, altitudes, nebulæ, Medusæ of gentle water, affinities of the ineradicable, passages over earth so eminently identical with incalculably numerous duplicates, alone in indefinite infinite. Do you take me? I mean that the pragmatic essence attracted self-ward dynamically but more or less in its own volition, whistling in the bagpipes of the soul without termination.—But to be natural passives, to enter into the cosmos of harmonics.—Hydrocephalic theosophies, act it, aromas of populace, phenomena without stable order, contaminated with prudence.—Fatal Jordans, abysmal Ganges—to an end with 'em—insubmersible sidereal currents—nurse-maid cosmogonies."

She pushed back her hair dusty with pollens, the soft

handclapping began; her eyelids drooped slightly, her faintly-suggested breasts lifted slightly, showed more rosy through the almond-shaped eyelets of her corsage. She was still fingering the ebony lyre.

"Bis, bis, brava!" cried her audience.

Still she waited.

"Go on! You shall have whatever you like. Go on, my dear," said the Tetrarch; "we are all so damned bored. Go on, Salome, you shall have any blamed thing you like: the Great-Seal, the priesthood of the Snow Cult, a job in the University, even to half of my oil stock. But inoculate us with . . . eh . . . with the gracious salve of this cosmoconception, with this parthenospotlessness."

The company in his wake exhaled an inedited boredom. They were all afraid of each other. Tiaras nodded, but no one confessed to any difficulty in following the thread of her argument. They were, racially, so very correct.

Salome wound on in summary rejection of theogonies, theodicies, comparative wisdoms of nations (short shift, tone of recitative). Nothing for nothing, perhaps one measure of nothing. She continued her mystic loquacity: "O tides, lunar oboes, avenues, lawns of twilight, winds losing caste in November, haymakings, vocations manquées, expressions of animals, chances."

Jonquil colored mousselines with black spots, eyes fermented, smiles crucified, adorable umbilici, peacock aureoles, fallen carnations, inconsequent fugues. One felt reborn, reinitiate and rejuvenate, the soul expiring systematically in spirals across indubitable definitive showers, for the good of earth, understood everywhere, palp of Varuna, air omniversal, assured if one were but ready.

Salome continued insistently: "The pure state, I tell you, sectaries of the consciousness, why this convention of separations, individuals by mere etiquette, indivisible? Breathe upon the thistle-down of these sciences, as you call them, in the orient of my pole-star. Is it life to persist in putting oneself au courant with oneself, constantly to inspect oneself, and then query at each step: am I wrong? Species! Categories! and kingdoms, bah!! Nothing is lost, nothing added, it is all reclaimed in advance. There is no ticket to the confessional for the heir of the prodigies. Not expedients and expiations, but vintages of the infinite, not experimental but in fatality."

The little yellow vocalist with the black funereal spots broke the lyre over her knee, and regained her dignity. The intoxicated crowd mopped their foreheads. An embarrassing silence. The hyperboreans looked at each other: "What time will they put her to bed?" But neither ventured articulation; they did not even inspect their watches. It couldn't have been later than six. The slender voice once more aroused them:

"And now, father, I wish you to send me the head of Jao Kanan, on any saucer you like. I am going upstairs. I expect it."

"But . . . but . . . my dear . . . this . . . this . . ." However—the hall was vigorously of the opinion that the Tiara should accomplish the will of Salome.

Emeraud glanced at the princes, who gave sign neither of approbation nor of disapprobation. The cage-birds again began shrieking. The matter was none of their business.

Decide!

The Tetrarch threw his seal to the Administrator of Death. The guests were already up, changing the conversation on their way to the evening tepidarium.

4

With her elbows on the observatory railing, Salome, disliking popular fêtes, listened to her familiar poluphloisbious ocean. Calm evening.

Stars out in full company, eternities of zeniths of embers. Why go into exile?

Salome, milk-sister to the Via Lactea, seldom lost herself in constellations. Thanks to photo-spectrum analysis the stars could be classified as to color and magnitudes; she had commanded a set of diamonds in the proportionate sizes to adorn nocturnally her hair and her person, over mousseline of deep mourning-violet with gold dots in the surface. Stars below the sixteenth magnitude were not, were not in her world, she envisaged her twenty-four millions of subjects.

Isolated nebulous matrices, not the formed nebulæ, were her passion; she ruled out planetiform discs and sought but the unformed, perforated, tentacular. Orion's gaseous fog was the Brother Benjamin of her galaxy. But she was no more the "little" Salome, this night brought a change of relations, exorcised from her virginity of tissue she felt peer to these matrices, fecund as they in gyratory evolutions. Yet this fatal sacrifice to the cult (still happy in getting out of so discreetly) had obliged her in order to get rid of her initiator, to undertake a step (grave perhaps), perhaps homicide;—finally to assure silence, cool water to contingent people,—elixir of an hundred nights' distillation. It must serve.

Ah, well, such was her life. She was a specialty, a minute specialité.

There on a cushion among the débris of her black ebony lyre, lay Jao's head, like Orpheus' head in the old days, gleaming, encrusted with phosphorus, washed, anointed, barbered, grinning at the 24 million stars.

As soon as she had got it, Salome, inspired by the true spirit of research, had commenced the renowned experiments after decollation; of which we have heard so much. She awaited. The electric passes of her hypnotic manual brought from it nothing but inconsequential grimaces.

She had an idea, however.

She perhaps lowered her eyes, out of respect to Orion, stiffening herself to gaze upon the nebulæ of her puberties . . . for ten minutes. What nights, what nights in the future! Who will have the last word about it? Choral societies, fire-crackers down there in the city.

Finally Salome shook herself, like a sensible person, reset, readjusted her fichu, took off the gray gold-spotted symbol-jewel of Orion, placed it between Jao's lips as an host, kissed the lips pityingly and hermetically, sealed them with corrosive wax (a very speedy procedure).

Then with a "Bah!" mutinous, disappointed, she seized the genial boko of the late Jao Kanan, in delicate feminine hands.

As she wished the head to land plumb in the sea without bounding upon the cliffs, she gave a good swing in turning. The fragment described a sufficient and phosphorescent parabola, a noble parabola. But unfortunately the little astronomer had terribly miscalculated her impetus, and tripping over the parapet with a cry finally human she hurtled from crag to crag, to fall, shattered, into the picturesque anfractuosities of the breakers, far from the noise of the national festival, lacerated and naked, her skull shivered, paralyzed with a vertigo, in short, gone to the bad, to suffer for nearly an hour.

She had not even the viaticum of seeing the phosphorescent star, the floating head of Jao on the water. And the heights of heaven were distant.

Thus died Salome of the Isles (of the White Esoteric Isles, in especial) less from uncultured misventure than from trying to fabricate some distinction between herself and every one else; like the rest of us.

POSTSCRIPT TO *THE NATURAL PHILOSOPHY OF LOVE* BY RÉMY DE GOURMONT

POSTSCRIPT TO *THE NATURAL PHILOSOPHY OF LOVE* BY RÉMY DE GOURMONT

"Il y aurait peut-être une certaine corrélation
entre la copulation complète et profonde et le
développement cérébral."

Nor only is this suggestion, made by our author at the end of his eighth chapter, both possible and probable, but it is more than likely that the brain itself, is, in origin and development, only a sort of great clot of genital fluid held in suspense or reserve; at first over the cervical ganglion, or, earlier or in other species, held in several clots over the scattered chief nerve centres; and augmenting in varying speeds and quantities into medulla oblongata, cerebellum and cerebrum. This hypothesis would perhaps explain a certain number of as yet uncorrelated phenomena both psychological and physiological. It would explain the enormous content of the brain as a maker or presenter of images. Species would have developed in accordance with, or their development would have been affected by, the relative discharge and retention of the fluid; this proportion being both a matter of quantity and of quality, some animals profiting hardly at all by the alluvial Nile-flood; the baboon retaining nothing; men apparently stupefying themselves in some cases by excess, and in other cases discharging apparently only a surplus at high pressure; the gateux, or the genius, the "strong-minded."

I offer an idea rather than an argument, yet if we consider that the power of the spermatozoide is precisely the power of exteriorizing a form; and if we consider the lack of any other known substance in nature capable of growing into brain, we are left with only one surprise, or rather one conclusion, namely, in face of the smallness of the average brain's activity, we must conclude that the spermatozoic substance must have greatly atrophied in its change from lactic to coagulated and hereditarily coagulated condition. Given, that is, two great seas of this fluid, mutually magnetized, the wonder is, or at least the first wonder is, that human thought is so inactive.

Chemical research may have something to say on the subject, if it be directed to comparison of brain and spermatophore in the nautilus, to the viscous binding of the bee's fecundative liquid. I offer only reflections, perhaps a few data. Indications of earlier adumbrations of an idea which really surprises no one, but seems as if it might have been lying on the study table of any physician or philosopher.

There are traces of it in the symbolism of phallic religions, man really the phallus or spermatozoide charging, head-on, the female chaos. Integration of the male in the male organ. Even oneself has felt it, driving any new idea into the great passive vulva of London, a sensation analogous to the male feeling in copulation.

Without any digression on feminism, taking merely the division Gourmont has given (Aristotelian, if you like), one offers woman as the accumulation of hereditary aptitudes, better than man in the "useful gestures," the perfections; but to man, given what we have of history, the "inventions," the new gestures, the extravagance, the wild shots, the impractical, merely because in him occurs the new up-jut, the new bathing of the cerebral tissues in the residuum, in *la mousse* of the life sap.

Or, as I am certainly neither writing an anti-feminist tract, nor claiming disproportionate privilege for the spermatozoide, for the sake of symmetry ascribe a cognate rôle to the ovule, though I can hardly be expected to introspect it. A flood is as bad as a famine; the ovular bath could still account for the refreshment of the female mind, and the recharging, regracing of its "traditional aptitudes;" where one woman appears to benefit by an alluvial clarifying, ten dozen appear to be swamped.

Postulating that the cerebral fluid tried all sorts of experiments, and, striking matter, forced it into all sorts of forms, by gushes; we have admittedly in insect life a female predominance; in bird, mammal and human, at least an increasing male prominence. And these four important branches of "the fan" may be differentiated according to their apparent chief desire, or source of choosing their species.

Insect, utility; bird, flight; mammal, muscular splendour; man, experiment.

The insect representing the female, and utility; the need of heat being present, the insect chooses to solve the problem by hibernation, i.e., a sort of negation of action. The bird wanting continuous freedom, feathers itself. Desire for decoration appears in all the branches, man exteriorizing it most. The bat's secret appears to be that he is not the bird-mammal, but the mammal-insect: economy of tissue, hibernation. The female principle being not only utility, but extreme economy, woman, falling by this division into a male branch, is the least female of females, and at this point one escapes from a journalistic sex-squabble into the opposition of two principles, utility and a sort of venturesomeness.

In its subservience to the money fetish our age returns to the darkness of mediævalism. Two osmies may make superfluous egg-less nests, but do not kill each other in contesting which shall deposit the supererogatory honey therein. It is perhaps no more foolish to go at a hermit's bidding to recover an old sepulchre than to make new sepulchres at the bidding of finance.

In his growing subservience to, and adoration of, and entanglement in machines, in utility, man rounds the circle almost into insect life, the absence of flesh; and may have need even of horned gods to save him, or at least of a form of thought which permits them.

Take it that usual thought is a sort of shaking or shifting of a fluid in the viscous cells of the brain; one has seen electricity stripping the particles of silver from a plated knife in a chemical bath, with order and celerity, and gathering them on the other pole of a magnet. Take it as materially as you like. There is a sort of spirit-level in the ear, giving us our sense of balance. And dreams? Do they not happen precisely at the moments when one has tipped the head; are they not, with their incoherent mixing of known and familiar images, like the pouring of a complicated honeycomb tilted from its perpendicular? Does not this give precisely the needed mixture of familiar forms in non-sequence, the jumble of fragments each coherent within its own limit?

And from the popular speech, is not the sensible man called "level-headed," has he not his "head well screwed on" or "screwed on straight;" and are not lunatics and cranks often recognizable from some peculiar carriage or tilt of the head-piece; and is not the thinker always pictured with his head bowed into his hand, yes, but level so far as left to right is concerned? The upward-jaw, head-back pose has long been explained by the relative positions of the medulla and the more human parts of the brain; this need not be dragged in here; nor do I mean to assert that you can cure a lunatic merely by holding his head level.

Thought is a chemical process, the most interesting of all transfusions in liquid solution. The mind is an up-spurt of sperm, no, let me alter that; trying to watch the process: the sperm, the form-creator, the substance which compels the ovule to evolve in a given pattern, one microscopic, minuscule particle, entering the "castle" of the ovule.

"Thought is a vegetable" says a modern hermetic, whom I have often contradicted, but whom I do not wish to contradict at this point. Thought is a "chemical process" in relation to the organ, the brain; creative thought is an act like fecundation, like the male cast of the human seed, but given that cast, that ejaculation, I am perfectly willing to grant that the thought once born, separated, in regard to itself, not in relation to the brain that begat it, does lead an independent life much like a member of the vegetable kingdom, blowing seeds, ideas from the paradisal garden at the summit of Dante's Mount Purgatory, capable of lodging and sprouting where they fall. And Gourmont has the phrase "fecundating a generation of bodies as genius fecundates a generation of minds."

Man is the sum of the animals, the sum of their instincts, as Gourmont has repeated in the course of his book. Given, first a few, then as we get to our own condition, a mass of these spermatozoic particles withheld, in suspense, waiting in the organ that has been built up through ages by a myriad similar waitings.

Each of these particles is, we need not say, conscious of form, but has by all counts a capacity for formal expression: is not thought precisely a form-comparing and form-combining?

That is to say we have the hair-thinning "abstract thought" and we have the concrete thought of women, of artists, of musicians, the mockedly "long-haired," who have made everything in the world. We have the form-making and the form-destroying "thought," only the first of which is really satisfactory. I don't wish to be invidious, it is perfectly possible to consider the "abstract" thought, reason, etc., as the comparison, regimentation, and least common denominator of a multitude of images, but in the end each of the images is a little spoiled thereby, no one of them is the Apollo, and the makers of this kind of thought have been called dry-as-dust since the beginning of history. The regiment is less interesting as a whole than any individual in it. And, as we are being extremely material and physical and animal, in the wake of our author, we will leave old wives' gibes about the profusion of hair, and its chance possible indication or sanction of a possible neighbouring health beneath the skull.

Creative thought has manifested itself in images, in music, which is to sound what the concrete image is to sight. And the thought of genius, even of the mathematical genius, the mathematical prodigy, is really the same sort of thing, it is a sudden out-spurt of mind which takes the form demanded by the problem; which creates the answer, and baffles the man counting on the abacus.

I query the remarks about the sphex in Chapter XIX, "que le sphex s'est formé lentement," I query this with a conviction for which anyone is at liberty to call me lunatic, and for which I offer no better ground than simple introspection. I believe, and on no better ground than that of a sudden emotion, that the change of species is not a slow matter, managed by cross-breeding, of nature's leporides and bardots, I believe that the species changes as suddenly as a man makes a song or a poem, or as suddenly as he *starts* making them, more suddenly than he can cut a statue in stone, at most as slowly as a locust or long-tailed Sirmione false mosquito emerges from its outgrown skin. It is not even proved that man is at the end of his physical changes. Say that the diversification of species has passed its most sensational phases, say that it had once a great stimulus from the rapidity of the earth's cooling, if one accepts the geologists' interpretation of that thermometric cyclone.

The cooling planet contracts, it is as if one had some

mud in a tin pail, and forced down the lid with such pressure that the can sprang a dozen leaks, or it is as if one had the mud in a linen bag and squeezed; merely as mechanics (not counting that one has all the known and unknown chemical elements cooling simultaneously), but merely as mechanics this contraction gives energy enough to squeeze vegetation through the pores of the imaginary linen and to detach certain particles, leaving them still a momentum. A body should cool with decreasing speed in measure as it approaches the temperature of its surroundings; however, the earth is still, I think, supposed to be warmer than the surrounding unknown, and is presumably still cooling, or at any rate it is not proved that man is at the end of his physical changes. I return to horned gods and the halo in a few paragraphs. It is not proved that even the sort of impetus provided by a shrinking of planetary surface is denied one.

What is known is that man's great divergence has been in the making of detached, resumable tools.

That is to say, if an insect carries a saw, it carries it all the time. The "next step," as in the case of the male organ of the nautilus, is to grow a tool and detach it.

Man's first inventions are fire and the club, that is to say he detaches his digestion, he finds a means to get heat without releasing the calories of the log by internal combustion inside his own stomach. The invention of the first tool turned his mind (using this term in the full sense); turned, let us say, his "brain" from his own body. No need for greater antennæ, a fifth arm, etc., except, after a lapse, as a tour de force, to show that he is still lord of his body.

That is to say the langouste's long feelers, all sorts of extravagances in nature may be taken as the result of a single gush of thought. A single out-push of a demand, made by a spermatic sea of sufficient energy to cast such a form. To cast it as one electric pole will cast a spark to another. To exteriorize. Sometimes to act in this with more enthusiasm than caution.

Let us say quite simply that light is a projection from the luminous fluid, from the energy that is in the brain, down along the nerve cords which receive certain vibrations in the eye. Let us suppose man capable of exteriorizing a new organ, horn, halo, Eye of Horus. Given a brain of this power, comes the question, what organ, and to what purpose?

Turning to folk-lore, we have Frazer on horned gods, we have Egyptian statues, generally supposed to be "symbols," of cat-headed and ibis-headed gods. Now in a primitive community, a man, a volontaire, might risk it. He might want prestige, authority, want them enough to grow horns and claim a divine heritage, or to grow a cat head; Greek philosophy would have smiled at him, would have deprecated his ostentation. With primitive man he would have risked a good deal, he would have been deified, or crucified, or possibly both. Today he would be caught for a circus.

One does not assert that cat-headed gods appeared in Egypt after the third dynasty; the country had a long memory and such a phenomenon would have made some stir in the valley. The horned god would appear to have persisted, and the immensely high head of the Chinese contemplative as shown in art and the China images is another stray grain of tradition.

But man goes on making new faculties, or forgetting old ones. That is to say you have all sort of aptitudes developed without external change, which in an earlier biological state would possibly have found carnal expression. You have every exploited "hyper-æsthesia," i.e., every new form of genius, from the faculty of hearing four parts in a fugue perfectly, to the ear for money (vide Henry James in "The Ivory Tower" the passages on Mr. Gaw). Here I only amplify what Gourmont has indicated in Chapter XX. You have the visualizing sense, the "stretch" of imagination, the mystics,—for what there is to them—Santa Theresa who "saw" the microcosmos, hell, heaven, purgatory complete, "the size of a walnut;" and you have Mr. W., a wool-broker in London, who suddenly at 3 a.m. visualizes the whole of his letter-file, three hundred folios; he sees and reads particularly the letter at folder 171, but he sees simultaneously the entire contents of the file, the whole thing about the size of two lumps of domino sugar laid flat side to flat side.

Remains precisely the question: man feeling this protean capacity to grow a new organ: what organ? Or new faculty; what faculty?

His first renunciation, flight, he has regained, almost as if the renunciation, so recent in terms of biology, had been committed in foresight. Instinct conserves only the "useful" gestures. Air provides little nourishment, and anyhow the first great pleasure surrendered, the simple ambition to mount the air has been regained and regratified. Water was never surrendered, man with subaqueous yearnings is still, given a knife, the shark's vanquisher.

The new faculty? Without then the ostentation of an organ. Will? The hypnotist has shown the vanity and Blake the inutility of willing trifles, and black magic its futility. The telepathic faculty? In the first place is it new? Have not travellers always told cock and bull stories about its existence in savage Africa? Is it not a faculty that man has given up, if not as useless, at any rate as of a very limited use, a distraction, more bother than it is worth? Lacking a localizing sense, the savage knowing, if he does, what happens "somewhere" else, but never knowing quite where. The faculty was perhaps not worth the damage it does to concentration of mind on some useful subject. "Instinct preserves the useful gestures."

Take it that what man wants is a capacity for clearer

understanding, or for physical refreshment and vigour, are not these precisely the faculties he is forever hammering at, perhaps stupidly? Muscularly he goes slowly, athletic records being constantly worn down by millimetres and seconds.

I appear to have thrown down bits of my note somewhat at random; let me return to physiology. People were long ignorant of the circulation of the blood; that known, they appeared to think the nerves stationary; Gourmont speaks of "circulation nerveuse," but many people still consider the nerve as at most a telegraph wire, simply because it does not bleed visibly when cut. The current is "interrupted." The school books of twenty years ago were rather vague about lymph, and various glands still baffle physicians. I have not seen the suggestion that some of them may serve rather as fuses in an electric system, to prevent short circuits, or in some variant or allotropic form. The spermatozoide is, I take it, regarded as a sort of quintessence; the brain is also a quintessence, or at least "in rapport with" all parts of the body; the single spermatozoide demands simply that the ovule shall construct a human being, the suspended spermatozoide (if my wild shot rings the target bell) is ready to dispense with, in the literal sense, incarnation, en-fleshment. Shall we postulate the mass of spermatozoides, first accumulated in suspense, then specialized?

Three channels, hell, purgatory, heaven, if one wants to follow yet another terminology: digestive excretion, incarnation, freedom in the imagination, i.e., cast into an exterior formlessness, or into form material, or merely imaginative visually or perhaps musically or perhaps *fixed* in some other sensuous dimension, even of taste or odour (there have been perhaps creative cooks and perfumers?).

The dead laborious compilation and comparison of

other men's dead images, all this is mere labour, not the spermatozoic act of the brain.

Woman, the conservator, the inheritor of past gestures, clever, practical, as Gourmont says, not inventive, always the best disciple of any inventor, has been always the enemy of the dead or laborious form of compilation, abstraction.

Not considering the process ended; taking the individual genius as the man in whom the new access, the new superfluity of spermatozoic pressure (quantitative and qualitative) up-shoots into the brain, alluvial Nile-flood, bringing new crops, new invention. And as Gourmont says, there is only reasoning where there is initial error, i.e., weakness of the spurt, wandering search.

In no case can it be a question of mere animal quantity of sperm. You have the man who wears himself out and weakens his brain, echo of the orang, obviously not the talented sieve; you have the contrasted case in the type of man who really can not work until he has relieved the pressure on his spermatic canals.

This is a question of physiology, it is not a question of morals and sociology. Given the spermatozoic thought, the two great seas of fecundative matter, the brain lobes, mutually magnetized, luminous in their own knowledge of their being; whether they may be expected to seek exterior "luxuria," or whether they are going to repeat Augustine hymns, is not in my jurisdiction. An exterior paradise might not allure them "La bêtise humaine est la seule chose qui donne une idée de l'infini," says Renan, and Gourmont has quoted him, and all flesh is grass, a superior grass.

It remains that man has for centuries nibbled at this idea of connection, intimate connection between his sperm and his cerebration, the ascetic has tried to withhold all his sperm, the lure, the ignis fatuus perhaps, of wanting to super-think; the dope-fiend has tried opium and every inferior to Bacchus, to get an extra kick out of the organ, the mystics have sought the gleam in the tavern, Helen of Tyre, priestesses in the temple of Venus, in Indian temples, stray priestesses in the streets, unuprootable custom, and probably with a basis of sanity. A sense of balance might show that asceticism means either a drought or a crowding. The liquid solution must be kept at right consistency; one would say the due proportion of liquid to viscous particles, a good circulation; the actual quality of the sieve or separator, counting perhaps most of all; the balance of ejector and retentive media.

Perhaps the clue is in Propertius after all:

Ingenium nobis ipsa puella fecit.

There is the whole of the XIIth century love cult, and Dante's metaphysics a little to one side, and Gourmont's Latin Mystique; and for image-making both Fenollosa on "The Chinese Written Character," and the paragraphs in "Le Problème du Style." At any rate the quarrel between cerebralist and viveur and ignorantist ends, if the brain is thus conceived not as a separate and desiccated organ, but as the very fluid of life itself.

EZRA POUND

June 21, 1921.

MUSICIANS: GOD HELP 'EM

MUSICIANS: GOD HELP 'EM

W HAT they don't know is the FIRST page of the exercise book. Namely, that a whole note equals a whole note; or 2 halves or 4 quarters etc. not approx but exactly.

And if I could DO it? That takes us back to Aristotle's *TeXne*, which the lecturing lice omitted from the curriculum.

Then there is the effect of counting in the English language, where *three* is a longer word, I mean takes longer to SAY than *one* or *two*. Hence that god-awful drag on the third beat in a four beat bar which has castrated and sunk so much British performance.

I can myself understand the complicated stuff, the theories, etc. If I could play two or four measures in time I shd/ be astounding the public from the platform. As it is I grope and try to warn others. Poor brutes who have nothing but performance to stand on, and who get started wrong.

There is, I am glad to learn, ONE piano school (address, Hirzel LANGENHAN, Schloss Berg, bei Weinfelden, Kanton Thurgau, in Switzerland) where the pupil is first taught that the PYANO is an instrument played with the hands. (Simple and one might think obvious starting point, neglected in institutions.)

Secondly the pew-PILL is taught that a composition has a main form and articulations, that is a root, a main structure, and details. To remember ONE main fact, and not a hundred separate notes . . .

There is nothing new in this doctrine. It is rediscovered from time to time, but taught inadequately, that is, it is taught in general not in particular.

Whether I shd/ apologize for beginning the preceding lesson with melody and not with the "first page" of the exercise book, can be debated. I doubt if any one CAN understand the first page until they are interested, I mean really and acutely interested, in melody . . .

When their hunger for melody and their melodic hate (as well as love) is sufficiently keen, then they may get round to noticing bar length, to disliking accordion bars which stretch and contract unintentionally, which are (in how many god damned editions) loaded with *"poco. rit."* and similar marks of ineptitude, in season and out.

And if the editor hasn't put in these indications in wrong places or all over the place, the purr-former performs 'em gratis and without indication.

After the first stumbles and the instinctive sense that a form must contain UNEVEN elements, one suffers and learns that an even measure if long enough, has room for all sorts of oddities and uneven figures and units.

This is a long time learning. People might be told, but would they learn it?

The learnèd and expert have such difficulty in understanding what the unlearned do NOT understand when told with an even voice.

Part TWO.

An open air show in this village indicates, perhaps, another chance for a little sanity. Lo Monaco (conducting), Anita de Alba, G. Guidi, in Rossini's Barbiere di Siviglia, emphasized in August various points that

Lavignac knew and that the public and bad composers have forgotten.

Rossini is, in this opera, unsurpassed by anyone I know of, in combining orchestra with songs.

This is not the same thing as fitting words to melody or making an unity of words and melody in a song or an aria, nevertheless, Lavignac in his condensed and insufficiently meditated vade mecum makes two points. First, that Rossini had told him that he (Rossini) learned his job copying the parts of Haydn's quartettes, and second, that Rossini STOPPED writing operas after his Wm. Tell (1829).

Which STOP, in the fear of doing something worse, was probably an act of genius, the master from Pesaro consciously or unconsciously refusing dead to participate in the general DOWN-SLOSH of the god blithering and bemessed ottocento.

England damned, since Cromwell brought in his usurers, to an avoidance of technique and of verbal clarity; to be obfuscation of all values and all honesty, lost the art of, and care for, singing WORDS.

That art persisted in Italian libretti, which are SINGING matter; which are NOT reading matter.

That art I did have the decency to notice, in "The Spirit of Romance," if I remember, in a brief reference to Metastasio. Or at any rate I have referred now and again to Metastasio. And there are probably fifty librettists who knew the job better than ANY of the bleeding literary gents who committed book-poetry in England from the time of Waller to the occasional heaves of Mr. Browning when he did an occasional lyric.

This technique, which includes and very largely consists in vowel sequence, COULD be revived by a hundred or so poetasters IF the term poetaster didn't exclude the idea of honest work.

The YOUNG have little to say. Adolescence is, in decent social orders, a time of preparation. Labour on the TECHNIQUE of singable words is honourable labour. God knows I worked in the dark from 1905 onwards, and the light has come very slowly.

I don't really care a hang about verse drama to be spoken on the stage. Anyway it is Mr. Eliot's job, and his fragments of an Agon are worth all his stage successes, but verse to be sung is something vastly worth reviving, and verse to be sung in opera, if it could be as good as Sterbini's in the "Barbiere" would be an addition to life as we suffer it.

It need NOT be reading matter. A great deal of Sterbini's don't even need to be looked up in the book of words for the simple reason that one can HEAR it when sung, I mean hear their words and grasp their simple meaning.

This note is in the nature of a prayer for the continuance of the open air opera in Rapallo. Damn Puccini, and my ingress into one other open air performance in another province only resulted in tracing Mickey Mouse to his lair in Boito (doubtless of historic and philological import but not part of my private agenda). I shd/ like to hear all of Rossini (to find out what is good) plus another hundred operas pre/Traviata.

There is nothing inherently impossible in their happening a few per year in Rapallo, or even in other of the numerous open air revivals now proceeding in Italy. The price here was from fifteen lire down to three lire, with voices audible over the fence for those reluctant to disburse.

The guild system is, or was from the 1st to the 4th of August, working quite nicely in orchestra in Liguria.

[By "accordion bars" I do NOT mean deliberate use of bars of SPECIFICALLY different lengths, that is, specifically measured changes in the great bass tone, but the undesigned and not specifically calculated playing off the great bass, as a bad singer sings out of tune.]

FRIVOLITIES

FRIVOLITIES

THE drop ploppeth
The slop sloppeth
The cold stoppeth
    My circulation.
The stove wheezeth
My nose not breatheth
Oh , J-HEE-zeth !!
    Flu and damnation!

MR. HOUSMAN'S MESSAGE

O woe, woe,
People are born and die,
We also shall be dead pretty soon
Therefore let us act as if we were dead already.

The bird sits on the hawthorn tree
But he dies also, presently.
Some lads get hung, and some get shot.
Woeful is this human lot.
        Woe! woe, etcetera. . . .

London is a woeful place,
Shropshire is much pleasanter.

223

Then let us smile a little space
Upon fond nature's morbid grace.
        Oh, Woe, woe, woe, etcetera. . . .

THE NEW CAKE OF SOAP

Lo, how it gleams and glistens in the sun
Like the cheek of a Chesterton.

ANCIENT MUSIC

WINTER is icummen in,
Lhude sing Goddamm,
Raineth drop and staineth slop,
And how the wind doth ramm!
            Sing: Goddamm.
Skiddeth bus and sloppeth us,
An ague hath my ham.
Freezeth river, turneth liver,
            Damn you, sing: Goddamm.
Goddamm, Goddamm, 'tis why I am, Goddamm,
            So 'gainst the winter's balm.
Sing goddamm, damm, sing Goddamm,
Sing goddamm, sing goddamm, DAMM.

NOTE.—This is not folk music, but Dr. Ker writes that the tune is to be found under the Latin words of a very ancient canon.

OUR CONTEMPORARIES

WHEN the Taihaitian princess
Heard that he had decided,

She rushed out into the sunlight and swarmed up a
  cocoanut palm tree,

But he returned to this island
And wrote ninety Petrarchan sonnets.

NOTE.—Il s'agit d'un jeune poète qui a suivi le culte de
Gauguin jusqu'à Tahiti même (et qui vit encore). Etant fort
bel homme, quand la princesse bistre entendit qu'il voulait
lui accorder ses faveurs elle montra son allegresse de la façon
dont nous venons de parler. Malheureusement ses poèmes ne
sont remplis que de ses propres subjectivités, style Victorien
de la "Georgian Anthology."

                                        M. POM-POM
        (Caf' Conc' song
                The Fifth, or Permanent International)

M. Pom-POM allait en guerre
                Per vendere cannoni
Mon beau grand frère
Ne peut plus voir
                Per vendere cannoni.

M. Pom-POM est au senat
                Per vendere cannoni
Pour vendre des canons
Pour vendre des canons
                        To sell the god damn'd frogs
                        A few more canon.

(Townsman, 1938)

ABU SALAMMAMM—A SONG OF EMPIRE

(Being the sort of poem I would write if King George
V should have me chained to the fountain before Buck-
ingham Palace, and should give me all the food and
women I wanted. To my brother in chains Bonga-
Bonga.)

Great is King George the Fifth, for he has chained me
    to this fountain;
  He feeds me with beef-bones and wine.
Great is King George the Fifth—
His palace is white like marble,
His palace has ninety-eight windows,
His palace is like a cube cut in thirds,
It is he who has slain the Dragon and released the
    maiden Andromeda.
Great is King George the Fifth;
For his army is legion,
His army is a thousand and forty-eight soldiers with red
    cloth about their buttocks,
And they have red faces like bricks.
Great is the King of England and greatly to be feared,
For he has chained me to this fountain;
He provides me with women and drinks.
Great is King George the Fifth and very resplendent is
    this fountain.
It is adorned with young gods riding upon dolphins
And its waters are white like silk.
Great and Lofty is this fountain:
And seated upon it is the late Queen, Victoria,
The Mother of the great king, in a hoop skirt,
               Like a woman heavy with child.
Oh may the king live for ever!
Oh may the king live for a thousand years!
For the young prince is foolish and headstrong;
He plagues me with jibes and sticks,

And when he comes into power
He will undoubtedly chain someone else to this fountain,
And my glory will
Be at an end.

"IN 1914 THERE WAS MERTONS"

In 1914 there was Mertons
A-sellin' Australian lead
For so much per ton to the 'ated 'Un
An' for twice that price to old England,
    For twice that price to old England.

WORDS FOR ROUNDEL IN DOUBLE CANON
(Maestoso e triste)

O bury 'em down
        in Blooms –
            buree
Where the gravy tastes like the soup,
O bury 'em down in Blooms –
            buree
Where the soup tastes like
      last night's
      gra –
        vee

O bury 'em down in Bloomsburee
Where the damp dank rot
Is never forgot
O bury 'em down
In Bloomsburee
Where the soup tastes like
      last night's gravee

O bury
'em down
In Bloos –
buree
Where the gra –

vy tastes

Like the

Soup.

"NEATH BEN BULBEN'S BUTTOKS LIES"

Neath Ben Bulben's buttoks lies
Bill Yeats, a poet twoice the soize
Of William Shakespear, as they say
Down Ballykillywuchlin way.

Let saxon roiders break their bones
Huntin' the fox
                    thru dese gravestones.

APHORISMS

APHORISMS

DEFINITION

Religion: another of the numerous failures resulting from an attempt to popularize art.

MENCKEN

did not overestimate the dangers of boobocracy. Unfortunately he thought, or pretended to think, it was funny.

THE VALUE

of criticism in proportion to actual making, is less than one to one hundred. The only critical formulations that rise above this level are the specifications made by artists who later put them into practice and achieve demonstrations.

THE FABLE

of the little girl who liked sunlight, so she pulled down the blinds, to keep it all in for herself.

231

APPENDIX

APPENDIX

CAT

HIGH on a ridge of tiles
A cat, erect and lean
Looks down and slyly smiles;
The pointed ears are keen
Listening for a sound
To rise from the back-yard:
He casts upon the ground
A moment's cold regard.

Whatever has occurred
Is on so small a scale
That we can but infer
From the trembling of the tail
And the look of blank surprise
That glares out of the eyes
That underneath black fur
His face is deadly pale.

Maurice Craig

235

NEOTHOMIST POEM

The Lord is my shepherd,
I shall not want
Him for long.

Ernest Hemingway

HOME-THOUGHTS, FROM AN OLD LAG

O to be in Brixton
Now that April's there,
And whoever wakes in Brixton
With glassy eyes astare
Feels the prison bars round his dusty soul
And the warder's eye at the Judas hole,
Whilst he carols out his morning trick
SLOP OUT: be quick!

And after April, when May follows,
And my whitethroat chokes with the muck it swallows!
Hark, where my sturdy guardian in the hall
Shouts to the roof and scatters on the air
Orders and precepts for the new day's call—
That's the wise dick; he does his stuff twice over,
Lest you should think he never could recapture
The first fine raucous rapture!
And though the floors are soiled with greasy dew,
All will be spruce when noontide wakes anew
The dinner plates with little edgeless tools
Far sharper than this world of witless fools!

N.B. I told my audience that I had to change Browning's
title, because nowadays A Broad, meant something quite

different, and I did not want them to think that I had gone to a Broad's home, to find out what her Home-thoughts were!

Barry Domvile

AUTUNNO

Autunno, quante foglie
se ne vanno col vento.
Vedi, nel cielo spento
la pioggia si raccoglie.

Tristezza vagabonda
di poveri viandanti,
pochi cavalli stanchi
nella strada profonda.

Brulichio de la sera,
vuota monotonia
porta l'Ave Maria
cosí senza preghiera

STAGIONE DI FIORI

E'il tempo di mandorle in fiore,
delle canzoni a mezza voce.
Su l'aia la fronda d'un noce
ripara le biade dal sole.

E questa stagione riviene
dagli stazzi con i pastori,
col suo vento, i timidi fiori,
cosí ogni anno e senza pene.

Ristora i teneri ruscelli
e inumidisce i biancaspini,
s'acciglia fra gli aghi dei pini,
ha il cielo canoro d'ucelli.

E' nata stagione di gioia
e non sa far nulla di male
perchè il sole fratello astrale
la illanguidisca nella noia.

GUIDES TO THE MONTANARI POEMS

Autumn, so many leaves
pass with the wind, I see
the worn-out rain
gather aloft again.

Aimless or vagabond,
a walking sadness, beyond
the deep-cut road:
horses weary of load.

A whirring noise, new night there
empty in monotone:
the Ave Maria
no prayer.

Time of almonds in flower
and songs half spoken;
walnut's bough now
keeps sun off threshed oats.

Time comes again
from the shepherd's pens:
shy flowers in wind
each year, thus, with no pain;

Renews the rillets, and dews.
White thorn, darkens in pine
with new spikes, a heaven of birds
sing to line.

Comes joy's season, that does no ill
for our brother the sun, aloft,
keeps it too languid and still
for any evil.

NOTTE DIETRO LE PERSIANE

Dietro le perisane ogni sera
gli uomini rinserrano
la loro vita
per morire una notte.
Ma c 'è pure chi sogna
un disperato tramonto
traverso i vetri e le imposte.
E chi rimane ancora
dopo ch 'è sfatto il sole
ad aspettare le stelle.
Sono questi i poeti
che hanno l 'anima di canzoni,
un anima tutta voce
e lieviti di speranza.

POMERIGGIO DI LUGLIO

La strada nella larga è tutto sole
e polverio di fieni, un acre odore
viene lungo la riva del canale
e l 'acqua del fossato che già sale
con la marea si tinge in rosso e viola,
E nel cielo una rondine fa spola
fra il tetto della casa ed il pantano
della carraia dove nel lontano
orizzonte che muore s 'ode il canto
di qualche spigatrice o un tenue pianto
d 'un fanciullo da un 'aia.

Saturno Montanari

When the light
goes, men shut behind blinds
their life, to die for a night.

And yet
through glass and bars
some dream a wild sunset,
waiting the stars.

Call these few, at least
the singers, in whom
hope's voice is yeast.

Road in the open there,
all sun and grain-dust
            and sour air
from the canal bank,

Ditch-water higher now
with the tide,
            turns violet and red.

A swallow for shuttle, back,
forth, forth, back
            from shack to
marsh track;
            to the far
sky-line that's fading now.
A thin song of a girl plucking grain,
a child cries from the threshing floor.

                                        E. P.

je l'ai surpris
à la lisière d'un bois
à l'aurore
le lycanthrope qui changeait sa forme

étendu dans les feuilles il dormait encor
et je vis un visage si plein de peine atroce
que je m'enfuis
épouvanté

Jaime de Angulo

DE ANGULO'S POEM TRANSLATED

Werewolf in selvage I saw
  In day's dawn changing his shape,

Amid leaves he lay
      and in his face, sleeping, such pain
          I fled agape.